THE PLIGHT OF THE BARBARIAN

"Stop him! Stop him! He has assassinated the Emperor!"

Valeron car Nadh did not have time to argue. *He* knew the Emperor had been dead before he had ever approached the throne . . . long before.

Right now he had to survive.

He stared at the Palatine Guards—the hand-picked, personal palace force. Then his left hand clapped helmet to head, while his right flashed across his waist to whip free his sword.

"YAAHHH Branari!" Valeron bellowed. His blade flashed down a man's face and clove his chin. Its wake foamed scarlet.

"Treachery! The barbarian has slain the Emperor!" The voice howled again, urging the palace guard on.

Moving with the uncanny speed of a man born and trained by necessity to battle, the Warlord of Branarius swung his sword.

The magnificent hall was becoming a chamber of horror, and everyone in it seemed to have one thing in mind: *Kill Valeron car Nadh!*

COLOR...ROMANCE...EXCITEMENT!

My Lord Barbarian

Andrew J. Offutt

A Del Rey Book

BALLANTINE BOOKS • NEW YORK

A Del Rey Book
Published by Ballantine Books

Library of Congress Catalog Card Number: 76-56150

ISBN 0-345-25713-8

Manufactured in the United States of America

First Edition: April 1977
Second Printing: March 1978

Cover art by Boris Vallejo

for once,
not to Jodie,
but to the ABC's
Poul Anderson, Leigh Brackett, Alfred Coppel
and the others of *Planet Stories*
—of loving memory—
for having helped make my adolescence bearable
and fixing firmly in me the notion that some day
I'd grow up (but not too much!)
and write one too.

Contents

ONE

Emperor and Minister

"Then Branarius is united under one rule at last!"

"Aye, Sire. He put all defeat on the main war-parties of the Sungoli and drove the rest far back into the hills. Rales car Shungol he met sword to sword, and did death on him. Now the Sungoli have pledged peace and their grudging allegiance to the man raised among them. They respect him."

The Emperor of the Six Worlds of Carmeis grinned in a manner most un-imperial. "I knew he would do it! And without the asking of aid from anyone."

"No, Sire," Elder Saldon said, and he added, "Now Valeron has been hailed Warlord of all Branarius. And he owes no other world—anything." There was pride in the old Branarian's voice.

"Warlord, is it? A barbaric title!" The emperor raised a hand to his full gray beard, aimed a finger at the other man. "But we all owe *him*, Saldon. Hope is with me that the Sungoli continue to give Valeron some trouble; else it's trouble on me that I might end in meeting him over shield-rims—or even yourself, Saldon, and the rest of you *barbarians,* in battle." The emperor's crooked smile was, if anything, the broader as he emphasized the word "barbarians."

The Elder from the long-restless planet called the Barbarian World bowed his head with its thin white strands of hair. Considerable scalp showed through.

"Valeron is a fighting man. He has a warrior's heart in him," Emperor Velquen said, in the respectful tone of one who himself had once been a man of weapons. "There are less and less of those about in these times. That young Jallad of Nyor, for instance; he spends more time with his Elders than he does on his throne,

1

and none, I hear, in working out with arms. Nor has he ever so much as been in the field." He shook the big head going bald under the six-pronged crown of plast. "With the Six Worlds united in empire, the task of *being* emperor is trying and dull for an old man who once wielded sword and ax."

The old man who was emperor over six planets sat back in his throne. His slightly squinting gaze was fixed reminiscently before him, down the long colonnade of marble caryatids to the immense brassbound doors of the throne-room. To them, and beyond them, and beyond the present.

"The gods know," he muttered, still staring past Saldon of Branarius, "that longing has often been with me for a sword again in place of this." Hefting the imperial scepter, he regarded it balefully. "And these," he said, tugging at the loose robes of sea's foam green reserved for members of the ruling house. "Thank all the gods for such men as Darcus Cannu, who are equipped with minds and patience rather than sword-arms."

Emperor beamed at prime minister, who nodded acknowledgment with a smile.

Darcus Cannu was smallish as Velquen was big, his face smooth-shaven in contrast with Velquen's bushy beard, his eyes an old-leather brown as opposed to his emperor's cinereous ones. Fifteen centimeters shorter than his liege-lord was Darcus Cannu, with more hair on his pate—a restless brown combed forward in monkish bangs—and the quick long-fingered hands of a man both brillant and ever-nervous.

"But there! I am at the doing of it again; talking like an old man. This damnable bald spot above a beard like ash is mark enough! Look at these hands, Saldon car Bredon; we are old men, all of us."

The emperor raised his hands for inspection. They were wrinkled, albescent, blotched and blue-veined with age, his manhood withering away with them under the weight of crown and years. With a frown, he jerked them down into his lap in the manner of a man who liked not what he saw, who begrudged Time its every depredation.

"What plans are with him now, Saldon, this young fighter with none more to fight?"

Elder Saldon shrugged. "First, Sire, to put assurance on you of his—our—unwavering allegiance to this throne and yourself." He nodded at the message-tube and scroll Velquen held. "My purpose here. And to build a greater Branarius—no, a *new* Branarius, a seventh world rising from the Barbarian World that was." Saldon's seamed face cracked into hundreds of fine lines with his smile. "He has chosen as his emblem an ancient bird of Mother, the phoenix."

Velquen glanced at Darcus Cannu. "What in Kroy's name is a phoenix?"

"A bird of legend, Sire, which rose from a chrysalis of ashes."

The emperor nodded with pursed lips. "Poetic and fitting. I'd wager Valeron never heard of one either, until Saldon told him. No denials, old rascal—and tell him I approve the poetry. For too long has Branarius been known as the Barbarian World." When he turned again to the prime minister, his smile became bantering. "It will cost us, Darcus. Money to change the flags and insignia, at once; a seventh world must be represented. A seventh place prepared at the Council of Kings."

"A necessary expenditure," Darcus Cannu said in his soft voice. "Taxes from the new member will soon recover our expense."

Saldon swung sharply to stare at the other minister, but Velquen was shaking his head: he spoke first.

"Taxes from a nation not yet built? Taxes from a people just rescued from constant Sungol depredations? Taxes from the one man in the empire with the edge to smash the Sungoli horde? No no, I fear we must wait awhile for taxes from Branarius, Darcus. Quite a while ... I'd wager Valeron hasn't even a throne yet." He turned questioning eyes on Saldon.

"Sire: he has transported to the capital the great black throne of the Sungoli chieftains The throne of Rales. It is carven of a single block of basalt."

"A black throne! A volcanic rock for the sitting of a volcanic man!" Velquen wagged his head anew and tapped a finger on Darcus Cannu's slender chest. "You hear? Cleverly he adopts the Sungoli's seat of power—more of Saldon's suggestion, I'd say. It is also less expensive than melting and molding out such a monster as this." The emperor banged a dappled fist down on the arm of the imperial throne, a high-backed immensity of seagreen plast. "No, I fear me we must assume the expense. There will be no taxes from Branarius for a while."

Darcus Cannu smiled his slender smile, little more than a rearranging of the muscles of his face. "Then in fairness to the others, Sire, there is no need for a seventh sword and seat to represent a world not yet a world, not yet a member of empire and Council of Kings."

Saldon's expression did not change—because with effort he willed it so. He was an old man, an ancient man in a time when newborn children could look forward to some forty-and-three years, if they survived the first; a man older by a decade than the emperor, who was thought to be fifty-and-one. Saldon was an Elder, a priest dedicated to service of the god Siense. His control he'd learned long ago, before Valeron's birth, while Darcus Cannu was at the knee of his tutor. It was with an emotionless face that Saldon looked at Cannu. He continued to stare.

"Tsk! Darcus, Darcus!" Velquen's smile was a gentle warning. "Uncharitable, in the name of fairness. I jest and call the Elder a barbarian, and he knows I do jest on him . . . but I fear he may think you serious." The imperial words were edged with warning, and all three men knew it. "But these are matters that we can discuss later with the—the Warlord himself." He shook his head over the title. "Saldon: please tell him that— No! Scribe!"

From between two of the female figures of marble that supported the gallery running around the great hall came a fourth man of age; the balding Carmeian carried quill and paper, and the inkpot swung from his robe's girdle like a badge. He seated himself on the red-carpeted steps at the emperor's feet.

"Velquen," the emperor said, gazing at the wall, and the scribe's pen scratched, "Emperor of the *Seven*

Worlds of Carmeis, to Valeron, Warlord of the Seventh: hail! Make that 'hail, old friend.' Umm ... 'Heartiest congratulations, both from ourself and on behalf of the Council of Kings, be with you in complete and final victory over the Sungoli, and your subsequent uniting of the tribes under one banner. The black flag which has hung so long here, representing Branarius, will be replaced with your, ahh, phoenix, as soon as one is received of you as model for our artists and seamstresses. Beyond doubt ... beyond doubt busyness is with you, building a nation and a world, but we'—no, change that to 'I,' scribe—'I wish to put eyes on you as soon as possible. Much have we to discuss over full cups. There is ... Umm. There is another here, too, with anxiousness to see you. Let it be said that is one of the important matters we have to discuss.' Umm ... sign it 'Velquen' and leave off all the titles and broidery."

The scribe nodded and left. Still wet, the letter was carried, gingerly, an arm's length from his body.

Gazing thoughtfully at his emperor, Darcus Cannu ignored Saldon, whose eyes were still fixed on the prime minister. Both men knew full well the meaning of the phrase "There is another here, too, with anxiousness to see you." The reference to her as an important matter for discussion between emperor and unwifed king/warlord held meaning for them both—and for Valeron, and the empire. Accustomed to priesthood and statecraft, neither man showed the effect of the words.

To Elder Saldon, High Counsellor to the Warlord of Branarius, the prospect of Velquen's sweetening an alliance with Valeron by making him his son-in-law was a splendidly portentous one. Saldon considered in silence.

Velquen had been a warrior once, before his blazing hair had turned to ash and begun to sift from his scalp; before his chest had shifted downward to bulge over his belt. Admiration and respect were with him for the young conqueror of Branarius, and Velquen saw in him a bit of himself, years ago. Too, jocular or no, his earlier words indicated some fear or at least apprehension of the virile young conqueror. The possible challenger to the throne would be handed it, effective on his fa-

ther-in-law's death! A man of Valeron's strength and
edge on that high seat would insure its being held for
the grandchildren of Velquen, who had lost both sons
in the Laviani Matter of seventeen years past. Thoughts
of succession and dynasty through his daughter formed
the only source of accomplishment and anticipation to
an aged emperor who had reigned in peace for sixteen
years.

The rumors that Velquen had cherished thought of
Valeron's marriage to Aleysha, Saldon thought, of Valeron's succeeding by that means to the imperial throne,
were true! With a Fourth Level exercise, Saldon composed his face against elation while he thought on it in
the silence following the scribe's departure. Saldon car
Bredon's barbarian liege had conquered the unconquer-
able, performed the impossible, led the unleadable,
united the unalloyable. The Five Kings would accept
him, Sungoli-raised and "uncivilized" or no!

Saldon's eyes remained on Darcus Cannu, studying,
wondering, seeking, watching the minister think. Darcus Cannu's thoughts were not visible, though, as Saldon's musings and his excitement were invisible behind
the inscrutable mass of wrinkles and lines that formed
the Elder's face.

Once emperor and minister had watched the straight
old man in unallayed tan pace down the long crimson
carpet to the doors eighty meters away, Darcus Cannu
re-introduced the subject.

"Sire: may I speak plain?"

"I'd not like you to stop now, Prime Minister."
Velquen gazed, squinting a little, at one of the milky
globes suspended from the ceiling; the eerily unfailing
lights of the Ancients.

Darcus Cannu nodded his head in a bow. "Can we
actually consider wedding the Princess Aleysha to this
barbarian warlord . . . *warlord!* Lord Emperor, the title
alone bespeaks the nature of his savage people! A man
who was himself reared by those Sungoli sons of Kroy?
A free-wheeling mountain edger who speaks no language save that of the sword and whose definition of

'make peace' and 'compromise' and 'rule' are all the same—'Crush'?"

Velquen's affable smile was gone. "Forgetfulness is with you that I fought side by side with his father. He alone came to my aid when I needed help, these twenty-and-six years agone. Forgetfulness is with you that we are *friends,* and you forget too that men such as Saldon possess tribal codes that transcend the ideas of justice and honor of us who are pleased to call ourselves civilized. Valeron has had yet no time, Darcus, to learn the polite mimes and lies and chicanery of . . . *civilization.* Can you hold forgetfulness that his father was a brilliant and honor-bound man—which is why he was slain by the Sungoli? Do you realize that Valeron has done something no one else—no, not even I—could do? How is it that these facts elude the mind I prize most?"

The slender man in the robe of deepest red-purple bowed at the compliment. "I have memory, Sire, that Va—the Lord Valeron was raised by the Sungoli; animals in the guise of yellow-eyed men. I have memory that he learned from them how to be adept at pillage and rape and mercilessness. A brute of a man, a conquering *warlord* with the manners of a savage and the untrusting brain of a fierce beast of the wildest wild."

Velquen was half out of his outsize chair. The old edgeman blazed up in his angry eyes. Recognizing that look, Darcus Cannu realized that he had prodded too far. Better to have waited, to have been more subtle! He met those clear gray eyes for a moment; then, not from fear but from shrewd intelligence, he lowered his.

He heard the emperor's loud sigh, watched his hand rise to stroke his beard, and knew of long experience that anger was being expelled with sigh and gesture. This was control approaching but never equaling his, Darcus Cannu knew.

Velquen car Velden had attained control, of necessity, once he had ascended to the throne—after defeating the man who had attempted to claim it on the death of Velden, Velquen's father. The barbarian might gain control of himself in the same way and for the same reason, necessity—but at what cost in the interim? The wholly mandatory self-control of a man who rules a warlike people on farflung worlds abandoned or "lost" centuries ago; could such as a Valeron attain it swiftly enough? Peace had reigned among Carmeis and its satellites for sixteen years, and within the Council of Kings. Saldon, Darcus Cannu knew and was thereby disturbed, possessed such self-command as Cannu did—and intelligence combined with shrewdness in addition.

The prime minister pushed his mind furiously. For years he had known that he was the more capable, more fit to rule than Velquen, though like Saldon he had fallen in behind the stronger and more magnetic man; Darcus Cannu *was* ruler! But *Valeron!* That hulking atavist deserved neither Aleysha nor the throne, and in all likelihood would not do credit on either.

Darcus Cannu waited, his legs taut, his flank streaming perspiration beneath his habitual magenta robe, for only he had discovered what Velquen knew not; in ancientest times, it was purple, not seagreen, that signified imperium. He waited, and the emperor spoke. His voice was ever quiet after he'd raised fulminous clouds of ire, and Cannu had learned long ago to fall silent and remain so. Velquen slowly recognized the reaction; Velquen calmed.

"Yes," he said, and slowly his minister's head came up.

Velquen sat well back in the Imperial Seat now, staring down the long line of snowy marble columns. "*Yes*. Valeron is an animal . . . a very clever animal, as was I. As was I—it is the only way. You can rule, Darcus, but you cannot claim and hold. Is memory with you of me, old friend, when first I came to this damnable seat of discomfort? I'd have had your head for such talk! Mark you—Valeron might too, now. It was the only way for me, and it is the only way for a Valeron car Nadh. Only a fierce animal of a man could rise from the Sungoli to best and rule them—and those wild Branarians whose loyalty has been only to their little tribes. They would sneer at Saldon, and at you too, at young Jallad of Nyor and his interest in the old knowledge of Siense. It is not enough to gain a throne—or take it. One must *hold* it.

Name me a better son-in-law, Darcus— No, do not. Time is not with us to go through the list of prospectives and strike off each name. And Darcus . . . there is an additional point, hardly without importance. Aleysha herself."

Cannu looked his question, and Velquen answered. "You have heard her, Darcus. She fell in love with him six years past, when she was but thirteen. She—"

"Childish romanticism, Sire. She has not even seen him in these six years. As you have just stated, six years past she was a child. It's little more she is, now." Darcus Cannu waved a thin arm in its flowing sleeve of archil-dyed wool.

"You say that because you and I are old, Darcus. Ah, blanch not at me that way; we are. Aleysha is no child. Aleysha is a woman. And he is a man worthy of her. Hmp! She may even be a woman worthy of him!"

"Sire: the princess has been reared here, in this palace. She has known gentleness and respect. Can you imagine . . ." Cannu hesitated, then decided to push it through. "Can you imagine that great brute in her nuptial bed? Your daughter?"

Velquen laughed. He laughed aloud, with his head back, boisterously. Again Cannu saw the warrior of old in his ruler, and knew then that there was no argument persuasive enough.

"Aye! Aye, I can see him abed with her! And I can see my silken daughter becoming a woman in one night!" And the emperor laughed.

The prime minister nearly shuddered. He was a civilized man and proud of it, proud of mind and station, a man with no time and little need for women. His face wore an expression now that he'd not have shown were his ruler's head not turned toward the gilded ceiling.

Darcus Cannu's voice came soft and controlled as ever. "If we must consider the princess, Sire, then let us do so as parent and guardian. Will he do happiness on her? He is hardly known for tenderness. And . . . can she, with her soft ways, keep *him*? He has never settled. His ah, bed habits are rather . . . irregular. How many offspring is it they ascribe to him? Fifteen?"

Velquen continued to roar out his laughter while

Darcus Cannu clenched his fists and his teeth. Slowly the emperor's head came down and again his gaze fastened on his adviser. The imperial eyes were wet with tears of laughter, Darcus saw with disgust.

"Probably a gross error in tabulation, Darcus. There's no such caution with him; there are doubtless more *cari Valeroni!* Gods, does a bride deserve—or want—a cringing, stumbling *virgin?* We should be hard put to find her one! No, you but add strength to the case for him, Darcus, because you remind me more and more of myself before I grew this hair on my chin to replace what I lost up here." Velquen tapped his naked skull. "And . . . think you I have slept alone these nineteen years since the death of the empress?"

Darcus fought to hold his outward composure. The fact that he slept ever alone was well known, and Velquen had twitted him on it more than once. "But you—"

"Wait," Velquen said, his joviality fading like the sun in winter. "As for Aleysha—come, admit it! We have spoiled her. All of us. She says there's love with her for him. She wants him. She is enough woman to keep him, and happy as well. She— Gods!" The emperor's face changed as he stared at the other man. "Darcus . . . you . . . is it possible that—"

Darcus Cannu smiled with all his skill. "Do I love her? Of course I do, old friend. She is your daughter, I am her guardian—and she is lovable by anyone. But chase that look from your face, Sire; you well know my habits regarding women, and too you heard me call her 'child' but moments ago."

"Um. I suppose I had best apologize for the thought, old friend," Velquen said, which was as close to apology as he came. "For a moment I wondered . . . you . . . and this throne . . ." His eyes bored, pierced as arrows loosed from a strong bow.

"The throne? Sire! Darcus car Nu stands as nigh the throne as a man such as I can, and yet breathe. I have no further illusions about—oh no!"

Nodding, convinced, Velquen leaned back, and Darcus Cannu relaxed as well.

"Dare I consider apology twice? I do. Umm. As for

Valeron, Darcus: the man is both intelligent and crafty enough to maintain a fine husbandly relationship with my daughter—if for no reason other than that she is my daughter and I am emperor, and nigh onto fifty-and-two, and I shall not live forever and else. Not with this stomach! But the throne *must* be held. The Seven Worlds *must* not return again to the throes of interregnum, to that awful time after the Wrath of Siense isolated us from . . . wherever the Ancients are. And Aleysha *is* a young woman, a soft and quite young woman, not a strong emperor."

"Then that *is* your plan! This . . . *barbarian*, ultimately . . . emperor!"

The words leaped treacherously from Darcus Cannu's mouth ere he thought, and he compressed his lips instantly. He had slipped, slipped, and Velquen was gazing at him. Staring. Was the emperor convinced?

Darcus cursed himself in silence, behind a face that had become a mask before the other man's cold stare.

"Good night, Darcus," the emperor said.

On the morning Elder High Counsellor Saldon car Bredon of Branarius left the old walled city with his detachment of thirty mounted edgemen in their blood-hued cloaks. He had done assurance on the emperor that when next Velquen saw the red cloaks and phoenix of Branarius, they would herald the arrival of its ruler. Saldon kept silent his wonderment on the absence of Darcus Cannu from this state occasion.

Refusing a palanquin and sliding instead his skinny leg over a horse, Saldon tucked the sealed scroll-tube into the folds of his dust-colored robe. He led his men out of the city at a sedate walking gait. The Elder gazed straight ahead, ignoring the stares of the people as he rode past, straightbacked for all his years.

They wonder if I eat children, he thought, and clamped his teeth tightly, damned if he would smile and have them accuse him of having bared his fangs. Composing his face as a priest of Siense, he reflected. *I wonder if wisdom is with the emperor in the matter of Valeron and the princess. Valeron will have much to overcome; what Carmeian could trust or look with favor on a Branarian, after our years of being the black-ban-nered Barbarian World? And Darcus Cannu—Valeron will not get on with that man long enough to remember his new-style name! Nadh's son might well be the better if I never handed him this letter-tube from the emperor!*

But he knew he would, and a short while later the Branarian spacer leaped up from the shipfield on a tail of shimmering air like that on a hot day. At the—fortu-nately—uncomplicated controls Saldon sat, smiling a tight smile.

Reduced to bows and axes, swords and bucklers and horses Man might be, he mused, *but still we ride the untiring shuttle-ships of the Ancients.* His eyebrows curved ruefully toward each other in the center of his forehead as he made the mental addition: *Though we understand them not!*

TWO

Minister and Barbarian

VALERON son of Nadh, called the Mighty, by the grace of Siense and Branar and the other gods—and by his own meter-long sword—Warlord of Branarius, expelled another curse with his breath. Another baleful glance he hurled at the great arabesqued doors of the imperial throneroom. Slitted gray-green eyes narrowed still more. His fingers clutched spasmodically at the black hilt of his broadsword.

Angrily he spun from the massive doors to stride, for perhaps the hundredth time, across the anteroom. Gleaming jackboots thudded into the magenta pile of the carpet without respect for the workmanship of the Mariole weavers who had made it over long years, painstakingly weaving into it their benisons and prayers and the one flaw they must, for only Mario was perfect.

A week ago, Saldon had returned to Branarius with Velquen's invitation.

Once Valeron and Saldon had discussed the emperor's apparent intent, the new ruler had hastened to turn over the reins of dictatorship to Saldon and Dernon. He had directed the packing of his best clothes—most of them but days old—and submitted grumblingly to a restless session with the barber Saldon sent, while Dernon chose the retinue of twenty men. ("Not the best," Valeron had instructed. "Not quite—the best edgemen might be needed here while I'm agone!") Those twenty, with his gifts, Valeron car Nadh watched loaded aboard his flagship.

But one man could have dragged him away from Jaksin, Capital of Branarius at this time: Velquen. And that on but one term: the possibility of marital alliance. That the emperor wanted to discuss such was reason

enough for the journey, but . . . with Valeron was a
flashing vision of a smiling young face, smooth and olive as was no face on Branarius, a soft oval nearly surrounded by filmy hair dyed the seagreen of the imperial
house.

Less than ten hours after Saldon's arrival, Valeron
and his retainers were sweeping toward the capital
world across the airless sea of space. Nor did the Warlord of Branarius give thought to what it had been like
when all space had been a known sea, when men had
voyaged among all the suns, when spacers were more
than shuttle-ships anciently programmed to pass only
among Carmeis and the six satellites the Ancients had
thrown around it like the spires of the imperial crown.

There was plenty of voyage time for reflection. Each
world was two ship's days one from the other, and each
was two days' passage from Carmeis around which they
spun.

The last meeting between the rising chieftain of
Branarius and the emperor had taken place on the
glassy surface of the Carmeian shipfield. But a kilometer away rose the sparkling towers and columns of the
city. That had been three years ago, as Valeron had begun the long Sungoli campaign. Alevsha—her he'd not
seen these six years. He'd been the fire-breathing *char-
ism* of twenty, a bare-armed, animal-eyed outworlder in
need of shave or trim and haircut both; she had been a
pretty thirteen-year-old peering at him from behind
draperies of plum-colored velvet that heightened the
pale strangeness of her dyed hair. Bade forth by her father, she had asked, in a just-changing voice, to feel the
visitor's muscle. Velquen but laughed while Valeron,
catching her hand betwixt bicep and elbow, had lifted
her off the floor and tugged her seagreen tresses.

Now she's nineteen, with womanhood upon her, Valeron had mused while he rankled at the dullness of
days in space. The Rites of Manhood were celebrated
at fourteen; a girl of nineteen winters was a woman and
more; Valeron knew grandmothers who were but
twenty-and-seven. One year older than he, though he
felt much older after three years and more of war, and

he knew he was considerably wiser even without Saldon—for whom thank Siense and Branar!

Yet fire he breathed still, and still he wore his tunics without sleeves to accommodate—and yes, to display—his biceps and powerful shoulders like uncrested Sungoli helmets. His greenish gray eyes radiated lines etched there by the sun and the cold and the dune-winds of rocky Branarius, on which something had gone amiss long ago when it was orbited. Now those eyes were expression-masking slits slashed into his face by month upon month, into years, of campaigning in sun and death and worry, and of poring over never-adequate maps.

(At that thought he made a mental note; cartographers must be put to work instantly on his return, and he cursed himself in two languages for not having thought of it sooner.)

Now he was a conqueror.

Now he was hero of Branarius and signally sure of himself. Now he was able to listen to others, and take heed. The orphan raised by mountain Sungoli felt quite the civilized ruler on his throne of gleaming black stone. There was even gray in his carmine shock of hair now, caught with a steel Warrior's Knot at his nape to fall loose and straight down his back. Now he had blooded his blade on the best edgemen of the Sungols, doing defeat on them and sending the pitiful remainder scurrying into the mountains to murder and rape and steal no more. The marauding tribe of Herkathon he had smashed and he had personally slain mighty Rales with his yellow eyes and hairless head. Now he was Valeron ni Thal, the Mighty, with a pale sword-line traced down the sun-etched swarth of one cheek.

Now he was Warlord of Branarius.

And Velquen had ideas with him of making Valeron his son-in-law! *Does the emperor have fear of me with him? Probably no*, he admitted to himself, with some reluctance.

The emperor respected him, admired him, felt some old bond with him, and calculated that he would make a fine warrior son-in-law; a valuable son to replace those lost in a brief and senseless war that was history these sixteen years. He represented to Velquen, Valeron thought, a fine alliance of strength in the event of dissent among the other worlds—or on Carmeis. None had trusted Vidul since he had done death on Lavian's king and seated himself on the wheel-throne . . .

Perhaps none trusts the Branarii! Or their ruler either, he mused, now he had formed the dangerous habit of conquest. There would be shield-talk, word-fencing, feints at treaty . . .

Thinking thus, plotting the course of Velquen's mind, Valeron had smiled as he hurtled toward Carmeis. He had no ambitions beyond building a mighty power on Branarius, where had ever existed naught save mutually hostile, constantly bickering tribes among the undulating jumble of red and ocher dunes broken by rocky cairns and shadowed over by the ragged mountains and scarps of the Barbarian World.

His goal? Valeron grinned and stared out into blackness while his ship flashed toward the capital world. To build a power to take its place among the other worlds of the empire, with high-chinned pride. To put happiness on its people. To found through a healthy woman a strong line of succession. What more could a man do? No thoughts he held of further conquest, no desire was with him to become embroiled in the around-the-throne politics of the Six Worlds.

The emperor will be surprised to learn that the very last place I want to rest these saddle-weary buttocks is in the Imperial Seat!

And then, four days ago, he had arrived in Carmeis City. And he had been put off and off. The emperor was ill; the princess was out of the city; unctuous tones and obsequy were honeyed with the pretty Carmeian pleasers sent each night to his room. None of it sat well, all of it rankled, and so he'd at last said, to Darcus Cannu.

Valeron was shortly thereafter advised that the emperor would see him next day.

Today. The day on which he had thus far waited three hours in this damned antechamber!

He paced. He glowered at the stony-faced guardsmen and at the rising paneled immensity of the double doors. The jingling of his—purely decorative—spurs was nigh the only sound as his boot-heels sank into the carpet's softness; he wore no mail. His brass-studded sword-belt he'd loosened a dozen times, hitching it higher on his waist when it slid to his hips. The line of statuelike janizaries stared straight ahead, making a fine show of trained sightlessness with their pike-butts resting on the floor beside their insteps.

Unseeing and unmoving they were, straight-mouthed and haughty in the cerulean tunics and white cloaks of the palace guard. A grin twisted Valeron's features: he entertained the delightful idea of swording into kindling-wood the big glossy table in the center of the antechamber, to see if the guards would come alive . . .

The grin vanished as he reflected. *Something is wrong. What—*

The towering doors rattled hollowly and swung inward. Darcus Cannu appeared, purple-robed as ever, a pleasant smile on his face. His bow was brief.

"My lord Valeron of Branarius," he said, "the Emperor of the Six Worlds awaits your presence." The thin man stepped aside and one dolman sleeve hissed through the air as he motioned Valeron in, with a flourish.

Accusation has been done on me of smiling without my eyes, Valeron mused; *this shielder is my superior at that!* Tucking his helmet under his arm, he stalked past the prime minister. Carmine cloak rustled and whispered at his boot-heels as he strode through the broad doorway.

"*Seven* worlds," he muttered in passing Darcus, without looking at him.

Ceremonial flambeaux set in ornate sconces flickered and cast wraithy light-dancers over the big man with the dark red hair who paced with long, swinging strides up the carpet. A full eighty meters from the door waited the emperor's throne, an outsize seat of laboriously re-melted and re-molded plast, almost clear save for a pale bluish-green hue, with a back nigh two meters high. Velvet padded that chair, which rested on a dais atop three steps.

Valeron's restless eyes examined the impressive hall

he remembered but dimly. The great room gleamed beneath a gilded arch from which hung the fadeless light fixtures of the Ancients. Those dangling globes had provided illumination for centuries. Never had they failed, or so much as dimmed. None knew their mechanism or the source of their constant luminous glow. 'Twas of the Ancients, and of inscrutable Siense, and the magickal lights even formed the center of worship of the Judlyn cultists. Here, the undying luminance cast a pale blue-green glow upon the dais and the trio of stiff Palatine Guardsmen there.

A long colonnade marched from doors to throne, each column an elongated woman of azure-veined white marble. Each fold and wrinkle of their carven garments, each chin and hip and breast was rendered with meticulous attention to detail. The Hall of a Hundred Woman; two rows of fifty caryatids set well apart flanking a central area six meters broad.

From door to throne the floor—not stone but the marless stuff of the Ancients—was covered with a thick strip of deeply red carpeting. At its end Valquen sat loosely in his throne, staring unblinkingly over Valeron's head. The thought came anew to the Branarian: *Something is wrong—what?* From behind him came the dry, toothy sibilance of Darcus Cannu's voice:

"Valeron car Nadh hight the Mighty, Warlord of Branarius."

Valeron hesitated, waiting for the eyes of his friend to shift down to his face. They did not. Frowning, he bowed. If this was the way Velquen would have it, cold and formal, so would it be. Time enough later to learn what had changed since the dictating of that warm letter.

Far behind him, Valeron heard the great doors crash together.

"Up."

Valeron realized Velquen had been ill; the voice sounded not as it had these few years past. Straightening, he flicked back his silk-lined cloak in an edgeman's automatic clearing of pommel. While he waited for the rather wan man on the throne to speak, one of the guards beside the great seat shifted his feet. The haft of his lance just touched the emperor's elbow.

The emperor moved.

Very, very slowly the veined arm in its sleeve of sea-green edged from the great chair's arm. It swung loose and heavy beside the throne, like a pendulum. The emperor tilted stiffly toward it as though the weight were too much for him. Then his face came forward.

Valeron started, stared in horror; the eyes now staring at him were glassy as the surface of the shipfields! Slowly that leonine head came forward. The hoary beard brushed lower on his torso. The imperial body began bending from the waist. Looking horrified, the guardsman who had touched his high liege-lord reached to stay him; too late.

Valeron took an involuntary pace back—and then hurried forward to catch the emperor as he slipped ponderously from the great chair to slump and tumble down the steps of the dais.

The Crown of the Six Worlds clattered and spun scintillantly, forlornly, to the floor.

Valeron caught the falling body with a surprised grunt; Velquen was *heavy*. Aye—and stiff, and cold! The Branarian's scalp prickled as he realized why Velquen had stared over his head, why he had not blinked. The emperor was dead. He had been dead before Valeron's entry! Now he knew why he'd not been admitted, why even an ailing emperor had not seen him abed, why he had been kept waiting day after day. There was a smear of cosmetic on his hand.

Valeron knew the grisly truth of it; Velquen had been dead when the Branarian flagship landed, days ago!

In his horror and furious reflection and his concentration upon the emperor, Valeron heard nothing until his arms were seized from behind. The Emperor of the Seven Worlds of Carmeis dropped at his feet.

"Lest you fail to understand, My Lord *Barbarian*, the emperor is dead. You did murder on him in a fit of rage, after he kept you waiting three days and then angered you anew." The mocking voice that chuckled into the Branarian's ear was that of Darcus Cannu.

Valeron froze and considered—for the space of two breaths.

And then the prime minister shot into the air to sail and flop ungracefully as his captive bent and jerked the light body over his shoulder in a continuation of the same movement that freed his arms. Darcus Cannu landed asprawl on the dais steps, with a grunt. Flopping, he slid down beside the corpse of the emperor he had so long advised and counselled.

With clinking of mail the guards came trotting down the steps. Lances came down to the drillmaster's Position Three: gut-point.

"Stop him! Stop him! He has assassinated the emperor!"

The guards! That was not the voice of Darcus Cannu. Gods, the Palatine Guards, the hand-picked personal palace force—they were in the plot with Cannu! It was Valeron they attacked, and crouching, he stared at them from beneath deeply red brows—for just an instant. Then his left hand clapped helmet to head while his right flashed across his waist to whip free his sword.

On the draw he sent one leveled lance aside; with a bound he avoided another. But he left his point behind, extended, and the Carmeian ran full upon it. With an ugly grating the sword ran up his cuirass, caught momentarily at fretwork, then plunged into the janizary's throat. Crimson gushed. Eyes huge, the youngish man sagged with his mouth gaping in a silent scream.

"YAAHHH Branarii!" Valeron bellowed, and gave his black-pommeled brand a twist before he freed it of the body and whipped it up in a blur of silver to beat away a vicious lance-thrust at his face. The clang still rang in the air while his blade flashed down the second man's face and clove his chin. Its wake foamed scarlet. He collapsed with a burbling yell, dropping lance to raise both hands to his streaming face. His third comrade-in-treachery was forced to skip to avoid the moaning man. Valeron's lashing heel crunched up under skyblue tunic and he brought his sword down with all his strength. Ancient-made steel sliced through helmet to halve the guardsman's head.

Even in that time of horror the Branarian edgeman's brain recorded information: the armor of the janizaries was primarily decorative; they were not expected actually to fight.

Now he heard the sound of pounding blows on the huge doors behind him, and he whirled. This time he ran along that scarlet carpet.

No sooner had he torn loose the bar than the towering slabs of brassed wood swung inward to sweep him several meters across the floor. In rushed a score of janizaries, now very much alive. Pikes and swords flashed, leveled to skewer.

These men saw a huge unarmored foe whose chest strained the cloth of his tunic and whose bulging calves knotted as he crouched. Born paler than they, he was dark red of hair and burned dusky by the winds and sun of his uncivilized world. Nor did he wear beard or mustache. Above the firmly set lips and large nose his eyes gleamed like greened steel through slitted lids. With a bloodied sword, he pointed.

"Treachery! Those men and Darcus Cannu—"

"The barbarian has slain the emperor!" Darcus Cannu howled from behind him.

For a moment pike- and edgemen stood confused. Then, seeing the body of Velquen and those of his bodyguards, they made their decision.

"Take him!" their prefect bawled, and his outstretched finger was aimed at Valeron's face.

Again a shocked Valeron car Nadh hesitated but a moment before moving with the uncanny speed of a man born and trained by necessity to battle. Again his sword, the silvery steel of the Ancients, flashed in air. This time the two men who rushed first upon him slowed their attack and lifted bucklers. As they split apart to converge upon him from two sides, the pikemen started forward.

The magnificent hall was become a chamber of horror. The white faces of the caryatids were grim daemons staring down upon the fugitive. The carpet's rich hue was but a grim reminder of Branarian blood to be spilt. Were they *all* traitors, paid in promise and clinking plast by the murdering prime minister? Valeron did not know, nor was there time to explain or question the men; whether from loyalty to emperor or ambitious slayer, they sought to kill Valeron car Nadh.

Alone of the men roiling in the great hall of Empire, he wore no armor. Nor did he hold shield.

His overlong sword clove the air in a semicircle of deadly silver. One Palatine sprang back, nearly falling; the other lost his footing and his sword, with an ear-assaulting clang. A frontal charge had saved the forces of Branarius's conqueror more than once, and he used the unexpected tactic now. Headfirst, he dived through the pikemen and sword-wielders behind them. How he wished for his gambeson of quilting and goat's hair and the mailcoat of Ancient steel!

As he dived he again roared out the old war cry of the Branarian Freeman in an attempt to freeze, even if but for a moment, the arms of his attackers.

"Yah Branarii!"—and he was sliding and rolling on the refulgent white and black parquetry of the floor that flanked the carpet.

The rushing man narrowly missed being skewered on the steel tip of more than one pike. But the long-hafted lances were unwieldy weapons at such close quarters and he rolled away free. Even as they came about, shifting their grips so as to stab downward, he was up and sprinting for the throne.

Back the length of the hall Valeron fled, and the red cloak streamed snapping behind him so that he put back a hand to still it.

More Palatines had come from the gallery behind the throne, and into their midst Darcus Cannu fled while the Branarian bounded over the stairs to the dais. He swung to face the charging guardsmen.

"Was Darcus Cannu murdered the emperor! These are his bought men; question and know the truth!"

"Captain Alerku!" Cannu shouted. "Command your force!"

"Take the Branarian."

Valeron's eyes became bestial lights. The commander of the Palatine Guard, the man sworn and entrusted with the emperor's well-being: Darcus Cannu's tool or co-conspirator!

In one bound Valeron was on the floor once more and snatching up swords from the men he'd felled. He hurled both at the mass of men behind the bristling tips of leveled pikes. Whirling then, he ran back up the steps and from there sprang to one of the four stairways that rose majestically in each corner of the hall.

He sheathed his sword, glaring about. Bright shafts of sunlight fell on him from the tall, trefoil-arched windows in the arcade behind the colonnade. At one of these windows Valeron now leaped from the staircase, knowing he must fall short. Below the window hung a draped lambrequin emblazoned with the imperial coat-of-arms; into this Valeron's fingers clawed. Stomach muscles became ironlike bands as he swung up to stand in the window.

For a moment his balance was in question. Calves cording, he steadied himself in the tall central arch, which rose nearly a meter above his head. He panted as he stared down at his attackers. He could not fight; there was no winning over a score of men after his blood for the worst of crimes, and him unarmored. It was flight he must seek now; he must reach his own men. These thoughts came swiftly while he surveyed his attackers balefully—and an arrow whickered past his ear from outside.

Clinging to the windowframe, he wheeled. The gardens, the far-famed Imperial Gardens, sprouted steel helms and longbows from every hedge! Palatine crests of seafoam green bloomed among the flowers. Another shaft, seemingly alive and singing, enveloped itself in his cloak and nearly took him backward from his perch. Valeron snatched off the lovingly made cloak of scarlet silk and whirled it about his left arm as a shield.

No escape that way—Darcus Cannu had laid well his snare! *Branar! How many bought men* has *the son of Kroy?*

The Branarian's eyes roved about like those of an animal treed by savage hounds. And so he was; and like any trapped animal he was trebly dangerous, without caution and possessed of and by incredible, hopeless-ness-induced bravery.

Out whipped his sword, to sever gold cords binding

seagreen drapes. The drapes flapped loose. Seizing their
heavy fabric before it could swing free to form a half-
curtain across the throneroom, Valeron kicked against
the windowsill. Out over the heads of his foes he sailed,
and they stared and cursed in frustration. Surely none
expected him to loose his hold in midair, doubling up to
whiz like a hurled missile between two caryatids. He
went rolling and tumbling, clattering and grunting
across the floor. Shock jolted his arm from its elbow.

The entablatured columns supported a gallery that
ran around the hall on three sides. Launching himself
to his feet, Valeron sprinted for one of the four stairways again, racing to outdistance a pair of intersecting
guardsmen. A sword slashed air with a *whish* behind
him as he bounded up the stairs to the gallery. Leaning
on the wooden rail, he sucked in great breaths while
again he glared down on upturned, inimical faces.

The marble women of the columns stared downward
with him, though their gaze was unperturbed and imperturbable. Their problem was their own: supporting
gallery and gilded dome. None helped them; they offered aid to none. Below, the rangy blackbeard called
Alerku yelled and pointed with his sword. Pikes were
discarded in favor of swords. The Palatines split into
two groups, to come at the quarry from separate stairways.

A mistake, Valeron thought. It was for the taking advantage of.

When they came pressing up the steps nearest them,
a snarling barbarian was there to meet them. Having
abandoned long-hafted weapons for closer fighting on
the gallery, they had placed themselves within reach of
a master edgeman's blade. That he too had erred in
trapping himself up here put on him no qualm or re-
crimination. None would pass.

With berserker viciousness he brought his brand
whistling around, wrist twisting in midstroke for the
backswing. The first man's sword and arm and shoulder
went flopping, spraying gore over his fellows. Valeron's
backstroke split a buckler and broke the arm that wore
it. Now they massed on the steps, pressed back from

the top and upward from the rear, so that they seethed like maggots in a wound. None wanted to be first.

One man was forced up. He swung his sword at Valeron's ankles. Valeron kicked himself upward and came down on the blade with both feet, while his bloodied glaive rushed in a silvery arc to tear eyes and flesh from the man's face. Desperately he tried to hack his way through and down—

It was from the other stairway that two others rushed him now, too soon. One he forced to duck while he smote the other on the helm with a frightful clash of metal on metal. Sword held; helmet dented to nudge skull; the fellow staggered against the railing. Without taking his eyes off the first man, Valeron bent and dumped the second screaming over the rail to the parquet floor.

An arrow keened past his head and keening in its wake came the voice of Darcus Cannu: "ALIVE! Take him ALIVE, you incredible fumbling IDIOTS!"

Valeron grinned, an ugly wolfish grimace that bared his teeth. A most welcome command! These man were not imperial retainers, they were Carmeians and Darcus Cannu's hirelings. All their passages at arms had been confined to the drill field. And they were to take alive the man who fought by no rules whatever save preservation of life through seeking victory.

The command had its effect at once. The man swinging steel at Valeron's head twitched his wrist to alter aim. Valeron winced and grimaced, for the swerving tip laid open his right shoulder, where he'd epected no blow. For a moment his sword faltered. Then he lunged forward and tested that man's cuirass by jolting his point through it with such force that he had to lay hold of the pommel with both hands to free blade from bone. The sagging, bloody corpse he grasped and whirled to hurl at the attackers coming at him off the stair.

His eyes blazed with the unholy daemonic fire that had sent the last of his planet's Sungoli shivering to rocky aeries. He chopped and stabbed and swung forehand high-backhand low and overhand, snarling, spilling blood down his arm with his exertions. For a moment attackers quailed before the onslaught of a madman.

"Yah Branarii!" he yelled, and his dripping brand flashed in a rush of blood-trailing death.

A man went staggering back into others, a scarlet gash across his throat gaping like a new mouth.

It was then that the well-thrown ax rang off the back of Valeron's helmet with a deafening echoic ring. Reeling, the Branarian fought to fend off the fall of purple night. He failed. Valeron fell to his knees and then forward on his face. The smeared sword slithered from his hand.

THREE

Barbarian and Prison

HE awoke to the sound of a loud, steady ringing. Slowly he turned his head this way and that, seeking its source before realizing that the noise was within his own skull. Setting his teeth and moving slowly, he touched the back of his head. His fingers found a long gash crusted over with dried blood. It seemed not deep, and he thanked Siense and the warlike Branar and Aria of Branarius that he'd had both helmet and shock of hair as padding. The ax would otherwise have sheared off his head at the eyebrows.

"A good throw," he muttered, with a warrior's respect.

His shoulder throbbed; there he found another line of hard dark blood. With a groan, he sat up—laboriously and slowly, with proper respect for a protesting head.

He had been stripped to the breechclout he ever wore, padded for protection and drawn snug under his stones, and they had left him his boots while dumping him into this dark little cell. His shudder was evoked not by fear or apprehension, but by the cutting chill of the dungeon. The air was stale, vitiated, finding its way in to him through a door that was a large metal grille; there was no window. When he leaned back against the wall, it was with a flinch at the chill of rough-hewn stone against bare back. His head he held well away from the stone.

Warrior's eyes roamed. There was no furniture. A pile of straw, gone sour with age and dampness, padded his buttocks and prickled at his legs. With a grimace, he wound up the recalcitrant machinery of his mind and set it to work.

27

The greatest warrior, the greatest ruler in a century—was dead. Murdered by a cowardly assassin with no edgeman's arm, a high forehead crowned with scant hair, a weasel's face and over-small eyes. Before, that face had been drawn, the eyes shrewdly narrow; Valeron thought now from a different mental set. Respectful dislike for Darcus Cannu had become hatred and contempt.

No, Valeron decided grudgingly, *not a coward.*

Traitor and murderer Darcus Cannu was, but no coward would set his feet on the dangerous road he now trod. The word Valeron ripped from his chest only heightened the pounding in his head: "Bastard!" Velquen had trusted his longtime adviser and highest minister above all others. That trust the snickering devil had repaid with death—*and he preserved the body that I could be made to appear guilty!*

Remembering the bribed Palatines, he smacked a hard fist into his palm with a slap that resounded in the little cell.

And now what? What, while he rotted in this filthy dark hole with wounds done on him? What was Darcus Cannu about? Did he aspire to the throne?

How? The Imperial Seat was become hereditary, no longer the prize of contests of arms—so long as the emperor met with the approval of the Five Kings. On her father's death, Aleysha succeeded to the high seat. Crowned or no, she was empress now. The prime minister? *He'll need luck with him*, Valeron mused, *to keep his stringy-haired head!* The prime minister, he remembered, was wealthy. That explained the Palatine Guards—if treachery on the part of the emperor's personal bodyguard could be explained.

But by the gods he couldn't bribe the entire army, and the Five Kings, to proclaim him emperor!

Could he?

No, no of course not . . . the armies of the Five Kings would—and then Valeron car Nadh knew he had the answer. He shook his head, as though physical action could negate the thought. Darcus Cannu meant to control Aleysha—either as guardian or—husband!

And the Warlord of Branarius? What had he to look

forward to? A quiet murder? A lifetime in this tiny hole? An opportunity to suicide honorably? Or would he be handed over to the enraged Carmeians? *Probably a trial before the Council of Kings.*

He envisioned that scene: the Five Kings, sternly staring at him. The honored protector of the throne, the twice-honored adviser to Velquen and the new and thrice-trusted Adviser-Protector of his poor orphaned daughter; the great Darcus Cannu would stand before him, doing accusation on a chained, scruffily bearded, dirty, shaggy-haired barbarian. The charge: treason, murder; the highest murder.

Velquen had ennobled Darcus, granted him a coat-of-arms. After this he would likely add a new device to his escutcheon: PROTECTOR OF EMPIRE, perhaps.

Rescue . . . The Branarians . . . Saldon . . .

There was no hope of their forcing way into the city, much less into this dungeon. Such an attempt would result in their deaths—and in Branarius's exclusion from Council, if not worse . . . and surely Valeron's murder lest his men reach him. Nor could Branarius withstand the combined strength of Empire when the laden shuttle-ships from six planets vomited edgemen onto its rocky surface.

Valeron cursed in two languages—then raised his voice and shouted into the dark. "HO! What about some ale here?"

His head pounded anew while his voice echoed out into the dim corridor and was assimilated into the tombish silence. What he wanted was water, not ale—but he had a role to remember. It was a part of his mystique on Branarius; Valeron car Nadh had never been heard to ask for water when ale or wine was available.

A faceless voice replied from somewhere without the iron grating that doored his cell.

"Shut your mouth, barbarian—you disturb our other guests. No ale's here for you—but *I'll* water you, when next Nature's urge comes upon me. Not another word, traitor—*murderer!* Bad enough these orders to keep my sword out of your guts, without listening to you."

The man would have been . . . mazed to learn Valeron's pleasure at his words. The Branarian smiled:

there were loyal men in the palace. This man shouted hatred for a supposed murderer, not paid devotion to Darcus. There was hope for Carmeis, for the empire *... but what hope is there for me in the fact that a man hates me as a murderer, rather than because plast coins have been put on him as bribe to hate?*

For many minutes he practiced the exercises of breath and thought Saldon had taught him, and when he got to his feet his head pounded the less. He went over to the grille.

"Belief's with you that I slew the emperor? You believe Darcus Cannu?"

"I bade you trap your lips!"

"Are you actually so stupid as to believe that hissing snake, or has he done bribery on you as on so many others?"

Boots clumped toward him and Valeron decided to be wise; he backed from the bars just before the guard appeared with naked sword. This was no Palatine, but a burly veteran who might once have fought, more than sixteen years agone.

"Wise decision, barbarian! Had you not stepped back you'd be minus a few murdering fingers. Now *trap your lips!*"

Valeron gritted his teeth. He raised his chin, swelled his chest. "Respect your betters, edgeman. Your kind I've let to victory scores of times; I rule Branarius by virtue of prowess. Darcus Cannu has murdered the emperor and done blame on me. Had I a sword in my hand you'd be talking differently; put one there and follow me!"

"*Rule!*" The man paused to spit through the bars. "Branarius! *Barbarius*, you mean. I'd welcome the chance, murderer. I'd *love* to face you edge to edge."

"You lie and know it, edgeman," Valeron said, continuing quiet and honoring the man with the warrior's title. "The man hasn't been whelped who can stand to me with a sword. Could you or your weasel-faced minister defeat the Sungoli? Did Velquen ever consider *you* his heir? Did *you* ever call him by name, to his face?"

Childish, Valeron told himself, *childish and stupid. This avails me nothing.*

"Attend," he said, with that dangerous quietude of voice. "Who you are I know not. But importance is with you because of what I am telling you. Protect the princess, no matter what befalls me! And when Darcus Cannu rules, when he announces himself her guardian or weds her, remember these words. Once they are wed she may not live long. If you wait that long in your blind stupidity, you have done treason the same as he. But you can at least avenge her and her father."

The fellow was frowning in thought. But he jerked his head as if to wake, and spat fulminously, "You his heir? Insanity's on you, bar—edgeman! You're not only a murderer—insanity's with you!"

Valeron glowered at him in the dimness. "Aye. Aye, you're likely right. I am certainly not smart—mayhap I am mad. Maybe Darcus could have done defeat on the Sungoli; he has no sword-arm, but that forehead of his is packed with brains. You're likely right—and loyal at least to your dead emperor."

Valeron turned away to sit down heavily on the pile of rotting, stenchy straw. His head throbbed.

FOUR

Prison and Princess

THOUGH many would not believe, the son of Nadh of Branarius underestimated himself. Not in the area of his physical prowess and skill with weapons: he was a brawny big man with thick corded arms and driving legs. Large hands curled around the hilt of an unusually heavy sword to make it a part of himself, a weaving, flashing, darting tongue of death. Too, unusual patience was with him, and it had proven itself an unconditionally valuable attribute.

It was his intelligence that Valeron ni Thal underestimated. His mind was the crafty, ever-alert machine a barbarian conqueror must possess, oiled with that patience that had been the death of many others less able to wait an extra few seconds or minutes. But Valeron *felt* his barbarism. It made him tend toward shyness. He knew his brain had never been refined, honed into the razor-sharp instrument he thought the prerequisite for an ambitious man without great frame and corded muscles. Valeron's was an intelligent though not brilliant mind; nevertheless he had devised tactics that had smashed foe again and again and were being put into writing, with maps and drawings, back on his little-civilized world.

Only a man of high intelligence could feel the inadequacies and uncertainties he knew when out of his own element, apart from his own kind. And so he took care to use that intelligence. His questing brain had just arrived at Darcus Cannu's remark of his first day here: "The princess? She is out of the city, my lord."

Could that have been a sneeringly oblique way of informing him that Aleysha would never be in the city; that she was dead? Valeron's eyes were bright with fury in the tiny cell. Yet of course with her dead, Darcus Cannu could not—

A silvery voice interrupted his thoughts. He bounded to his feet at the rattle of a hand on the grille and was across the cell in two long strides. She was an olive face and two slim hands surrounded by hood and floor-trailing skirts of a cloak whose color was the brown of mourning.

"Aleysha!"

She raised a cautioning finger to her lips. "Softly. One guard I know is mine, but there are others. Nor can I put trust in any."

"Bribed?"

"Not with plast. Nor with myself, my lord Valeron. I have women who are loyal to me."

He resolved to make sure that his Branarians were well paid and well watched and never over-tight of stones; these Carmeians were too easy prey! "What has Darcus Cannu said of me?"

"That—that you did death on father." He saw the bright glisten of tears, even in the prison's shadowed grayness. "That he kept you waiting several days, then insulted you when finally he admitted you. You lost your temper and slew him in an insane rage. Valeron . . . he says that father told you you were a fool to have thoughts of you and me, that he had promised me to . . . Darcus. I—you wanted the throne, through me, and said so . . . and slew berserkish when he told you of Darcus."

Valeron tightened his lips around a curse. His voice he check-reined. "And what do you believe, lady Princess?"

"Not that my father kept you waiting, or insulted you either. Captain Alerku and his men upheld Darcus. Much thought had been with me. I do not believe. They must be Darcus's men, now."

"The Palatine Prefect himself! His name and face I'll not forget. And the rest . . . what believe you, Aley—lady Princess?"

"I am here."

He strained to see into her tear-filled eyes. "When . . . was the last time you . . . saw him, alive?"

She choked back a sob, deep in her throat. She was but a face, an oval face below hair dyed like the foam of the sea that peeped from her hood; a face afloat above an ungirt robe of drab that fell from throat to instep. "Over a week ago. I—I have been visiting King Eshara on Sid-Alors. Father sent me; I suppose he expected you and thought it best I was not here, at first?"

Aye, Valeron thought sourly. With a little suasion from Darcus Cannu, the emperor had decided Aleysha was better offworld during discussion of her as part of the goods of agreement.

"Aleysha: I believe he was slain the same day I arrived. I was kept waiting that they might patch up a motive. And the lie of your father's plan to wed you to Darcus ... oh, it's an excellent and believable case against me, a *barbarian*. This was planned well. Planned well." He wheeled from her to pace his cubicle, eyes on the floor. "What is that son of Kroy about now?"

"Sureness is not with me. I think he means to—to ask permission of the kings to conduct your trial out of Council."

Again Valeron snarled a filthy oath, in Sungoliye. He swung back to her. "Aleysha: the throne is yours, now."

Dark hood shook back and forth. "Not really. The coronation is tomorrow morning at the fifth."

"So early!"

"Aye. Darcus has scheduled it early, and plans to contact the Five Kings after. You he hopes to keep here, and them there—I am helpless. I am little less prisoner than you. I cannot even depart the city, much aside reach one of the other worlds."

"And so to remain, so long as I am here. Realization is with you that you're in danger?"

"I ... think not. Not, at least, for ... two weeks." Her voice was low and quiet, its silvery quality restrained by helplessness and grief. "Darcus has announced our ... wedding, in two weeks. He claims was father's wish, and that mourning not postpone his wish." She managed to strangle another sob at her lips.

"If your father had a last wish, Aleysha ca Velquain,

it was that Darcus Cannu be bled like a hog at slaugh-
ter-time! Two weeks! Then we have that long. Aleysha:
I have never run from a fight. But I must get off Carmeis."

"I know." She turned away and bent. Cloth rustled
before she turned back to him with a slim leather
sheath on her palm. "For that reason I brought this."

He accepted the nasty little dagger in silence, slipping
it half out of its sheath to see the wicked triangular
blade of a poniard. He kept her hand. The fingers were
cold, cold and tiny and soft, unlike the hands of the
women of his brawling world.

"I'm left no place to hide it," he said, and his teeth
flashed in a near-smile that was little more than a wolfish skinning of lips from teeth. He glanced down at the
high-sided loincloth that was his only clothing. She
dropped her head.

This is a regal and soft woman, he thought. *No Branarian wench—not even a Branarian noblewoman!—
would look away from a man's nakedness, much aside
his near-nakedness!*

"Valeron: sorrow's with me—but I can't *do* anything
more! The army, the palace staff—are *his.* Oh, loyalty's
with some, surely—but I know not which, and none
will believe you innocent without some sort of proof.
They—thev'd have thought with them that I was put-
ting—" her eyes dropped—"personal feelings above
the good of Empire, above even love of father. He—"

"Have you knowledge that is not true?"

Her eyes searched the darkness for his. "I . . . no."

The word affected him more than could have an impassioned swearing that she was thinking only of Empire—or that he'd been not out of her thoughts these
six years. She had given him answer, in a hesitation and
a word, and he tightened his fingers on hers while he
seized her other hand. The bars were cold.

"He must have me alive," she said. "At least until we
are wed." The word emerged between her lips like a
piece of wormy fruit. "I have no one to help—no one I
can trust."

"You have. This is enough." He slid the sheath into
his loincloth, behind. "But it may mean the death of

someone loyal to you. You are certain? Certain you want me free to rouse trouble for Darcus—possibly civil war?" His hand touched, through the bars, the pale-dyed silk of her hair.

"I am certain. Of course."

Damning the bars, he pulled her against them and managed a half-kiss of lips that remained soft under his. "Until I can do better. Where shall I go?"

Neither admitted any consideration of the possibility he might not gain freedom of the prison. "My old room," she said. "Across the hall from ... from father's room. It is being watched, but no man will come in there. Those rooms have been inviolate to men for over a century."

He forced a grim smile. "Be sure to extinguish the lights when you prepare for bed. I'll come there, Aleysha. *After* your crowning. You put no value with the guards? Not one?"

"I cannot be *sure,* Valeron. Not of a single one."

He shook his head and cracked fist into palm. Her hands waited passively for the return of his. "What hour is it, Aleysha?"

"Now? Sometime after the eighth."

"Of what day? How long have I been down here?"

"Over forty hours."

"Siense! In this damned rathole there's no night or day! What of my men?"

"Prisoners, with no harm done them. Valeron, I must go. I—"

"Tell me about the guard. Tell me so I will know when it is night, and no one will bring me food."

"The guard down here changes each five hours. I'm—I'm afraid to stay ... afraid to go ... *No!* No, I am not."

"Good. That's it. Keep courage with you, Aleysha—*up*stairs."

She pressed his hands. "Siense maintain his light on you."

"And on you, Empress."

He watched her back as she slipped away to disappear into the grayness of the dungeon. That damned drab robe—what did Aleysha look like, at nineteen?

What had she become? The daughter of the emperor! Aye, she'd surely changed in these six years; a woman now, and a lovely one. The slim angularity of her body must have changed, too. In the darkling cell, he grinned. He'd soon know! He'd learn the soft body that went with those soft, waiting-to-be-covered hands and those impassive velvet lips. He'd know her, explore her, roam her.

Already he was assuming that he was free, free to examine her more closely in better light. The pale seagreen hair cascading over and well past her little round shoulders; the startling tawny eyes; that tiny purple mouth. How different Aleysha was from the women of Branarius! Barbarians they, frank and lusty, making known their wants and working as hard at the making of love as their uncouth men. His own concubines were carefully chosen for beauty of face and body; he had a weakness on him for big jumpy breasts and luxurious hips and pronounced bellies, all with their appearance of childbearing ability. But—the daughter of an emperor! A symbol of civilization and culture . . .

Love was something he knew not and had never known. Perhaps now. He was a hard man, driven by his own animal-fire. There had been no place and no time for love in his life, nor was such the way of the Sungoli, who had raised him as one of theirs. He barely remembered, in savage sweating dreams, how at three he had seen his mother and father slain by the hairless men of Sungol. Him they had taken to rear among the cairns and slopes of southward Branarius.

They raised me as Sungol. Love is a word I heard when I'd left them.

Yet he had been ever different. He'd had to do more to prove himself, just a little more than the other boys, the hairless boys who called him ugly and made fun that his eyes were not golden. At fifteen they had wed him to a Sungoli maid with great golden eyes and a body that betrayed her and destroyed their foetus of two months. At sixteen he had fled "his" tribe and rejoined his own people. Still he was different, and only just accepted. Again he had been unknown and untrusted, a man apart. He was called names and stared at and whispered about. He'd had to prove himself anew and repeatedly.

And then he became the Sungoli-killing machine, a man dedicated to ridding his planet of those who'd slain his parents and kept him different and apart all his years; those who were half-animals from none knew of what dark corner of Branarius or space. He had known no father; Branarius and his own people became Father and he slew for them. He had no mother; he remained a lonely man with a weakness for women who had the appearance of motherhood.

His following grew. None knew Sungoli ways better than the burly loner with the Sungoli name that twisted the tongue. None could better out-think them than the man called Valeron who slew a man, slew him with bare, cording, squeezing hands, for calling him contemptuously by his Sungoli name. They followed him, him and the flashing, living sword forged of Ancient-steel. It was they who called his sword *Jimarah*, blood-drinker, they who named him *ni Thal*, the Mighty; they who later called him Warlord.

More followed him, until all the people of the small, artificially orbited world followed him. With high impatience they waited while he journeyed to Carmeis on one of the ships they used without understanding its mechanisms. Back he came, with an imperial banner to carry against the Sungoli in the final, vicious battles among the rugged gorges and dark brows of mountainous terrain as fierce in hostility as they. Jagged volcanic rocks with their jutting basaltic ramparts became a blood-drenched tomb, one great tomb for the Sungoli who had so long raided and terrorized where they would.

The man whose *other* name was whispered but never spoken aloud had become a tribal leader and then a national leader where there was no nation and then a world leader in the holy war to secure Branarius for the Branarians. Quite naturally he had taken his women where he found them, finding it so easy he had never given thought on it; they hurled themselves at the living folk-hero with bellies yearning to bear his sons. Camp and later dark-stoned castle he had stocked with their big-bosomed, broad-hipped legion.

Now, in the dismal cubicle of cinereous stone beneath the Imperial Palace in Carmeis City, he decided it was time he learned other and else; time he made other investigations. It was civilization he must bring Branarius.

What was love? How was it practiced amid the polished and cushioned softness of civilization and its satin women? He realized, listening to the slither of Aleysha's soft-booted feet as she ascended the steps, that he had a high new mission. To become a civilized man and to bring home to Branarius the culture of the Six Worlds, the worlds that before the Wrath—some said—had used the seventh planet as their penal world.

Thousands of years before his birth, victorious men of the same passions and fierce fighting strength had known nigh-identical thoughts. They had conquered and looked upon the cultured beauty of Achaea. Liking it, they scooped it up to carry home to Rome.

And how better, Valeron mused, than through the heiress to the throne of the Six—*Seven*—Worlds? That would certainly be bringing home to his harsh planet the soft delicacy of the thing men called culture: civilization. He grinned the wolf's grin. And she had come to him! She had brought him her own gemmed dagger to help effect his escape! Now all he must do was stab and beat his way out of this stinking hole, rally forces to crush Darcus Cannu and his traitorous sycophants, and claim the girlish empress.

All!

Valeron car Nadh relaxed as best he could on the straw, and attempted to form workable plans. *All!*

FIVE

Poniard and Glaive

INTERMINABLE minutes of dismal darkness dragged on like hours, to become hours that were like weeks. The Warlord of Branarius alternated pacing with lounging—not quite comfortably—on the pile of straw. The guard changed, and changed again. At last with a new sentry came a bent old fellow with food and a bit of water. Contrary to Valeron's expectations, the food was not at all bad—save that there was not enough of it.

The old man left. Valeron heard, somewhere, the closing crash of the door leading into the dungeon. The sentry, having made rounds with the old servant, lounged past and disappeared from sight. Valeron waited. Occasionally the murk-deepened silence of the place was ripped apart by an awful scream or a laugh of lunacy; more than one prisoner had lost his mind down here. A gibbering came too, and a moaning, in a woman's voice. And snoring.

Valeron waited.

At last he wet his face with his carefully saved ration of water, and slowly and carefully used Aleysha's dagger to scrap the stubble from his face. To a man unaccustomed to hot water, to fine-honed razors, to smoothing soap and cremes, a man whose face was burned and leathered by wind and sun and slashing sand, shaving with poniard and cold water was no horrid task. If he was to escape, to make his way out of this place and indeed the palace, his stubble was a deterrent to any disguise.

"What hour is it?"

His voice rang hollowly in the dungeon and he failed miserably to sound subdued. He was not accustomed to

40

it. The little knife he tucked back into his loincloth, its
sheath nestling uncomfortably between his buttocks. He
was forced to repeat the question before a weavy voice
asked—after a hideous shriek from another mad
prisoner:

"What care have you for the time, dead man?"

"I ask to learn whether it's morning, that I'll know
whether to wake."

The voice laughed. "You are a cool enough one! It's
night on us now, barbarian, and the rest of your fellow
guests are trying to sleep. Tomorrow is a big and busy
day."

"I wish you fellows would tell us. Evidently I slept of
the afternoon, and now there's no tiredness with me."
Valeron slipped a confidential tone into his voice.
"Come closer, will you? I have a confidential question."

"Ask from there, big one. I've seen you fight."

Ah; this was one of Darcus Cannu's paid traitors,
one of those who'd been in the throne-room. "Forget
it," Valeron said. "I'll query the next man, unless he
too has fear with him, of an unarmed man in a locked
cell."

Valeron listened to silence. Then the clank of metal
harness and the creak of leather sounded, with the thud
of booted feet. The Branarian smiled; he'd been successful in piquing the man's curiosity and pride.
Pressing back into the gloom to the right of the barred
door, he held his breath. The footsteps stopped.

"Oh no, barbarian. Not till I can lay eyes on you.
Surely you take me not for the sort of fool who will
poke in his head to see where you are, and find out too
late!" The guard's laugh was scornful.

Valeron bit off an oath; aye, that was exactly what
he'd hoped. He slid along the wall and stepped out into
the center of his cell.

"No, I want knowledge of something." He grinned.
"The princess." He had lowered his voice; the grin was
lecherous.

Again the Carmeian laughed. "A *lot* of us would like
knowledge with us of her, Branarian! But you can be
certain you and I will never learn—old Darcus will!"

Valeron turned away. "Now that is what I call

waste," he said, and gave ear to the sound of two foot-steps as the fellow came closer to the door. "It's doubt I have with me whether the son of Nu has the necessary equipment."

Still again the guard laughed, not scornfully this time, but conspiratorially. No such fool was he as to come close to a dangerous prisoner. But the outworlder was well across the cell, now, and it was obvious that only the desire to talk was with him—and about a pleasant topic at that.

"You *are* a cool one, Branarian. I make admission that since it can't be me, I'd rather see *you* breach that maidenly wall than D—"

Valeron's hand had already slid the dagger from its sheath. Now he spun and rushed in a move that was far too fast for anyone save a desert-mountain man reared by the Sungoli. His knees bent and straightened, propelling him across the cubicle even while he turned. One arm drove through the bars, and he paid no heed to the painful scraping as he circled a helmeted head with that clamping arm. The other shot through with fisted hand, to tickle a Carmeian adam's apple with the point of Aleysha's poniard. The gems in the hilt winked in the light from the sentry's torch. He dropped it; it sputtered at his feet.

"Make no shout. Open the door. Quick!"

"I—I have no keys—"

"You were not so stupid as to come near the door, have memory? Nor am I stupid enough to believe that. If you do *not* have the keys, I may as well do death on you." He exerted pressure on the slim, triangular-bladed knife.

Keys rattled and jangled. The grille swung slowly outward—and the Carmeian tore loose. He danced back, his sword *wheep*ing from its scabbard.

A long leap carried Valeron out into the corridor, facing the extended point of that sword. Foolish, that; his hand went back over his shoulder and snapped forward as the guardsman opened his mouth to call an alarm.

Valeron was no expert, nor was the dagger a throwing knife; its jeweled hilt made it handle-heavy. It went high, hilt forward, and the crosspiece raked the other man's face under one eye. As he staggered back, blinking, a pouncing Valeron's balled fist smashed his face. The Carmeian fell without a cry. The sword clattered across the stones.

Valeron donned the man's white cloak and sky-colored tunic, strained to fasten the light ornamental cuirass about himself, and buckled on the sword-belt. Retrieving the broadsword, he shoved it home in the scabbard. The helmet with its bobbing imperial panache of seagreen was too tight—the Palatines wore their hair ludicrously short—but he pressed it down over his head and fastened the chin strap once he'd let it out a bit. The guard's own underclothing served to mop the blood from the ruined face, after he'd dragged the man into the cell.

The Palatine still breathed; even through that slivered paste of skin and blood and bone he could cry out once he regained consciousness. And this man had been among those in the great hall; he was a traitor in Darcus Cannu's employ. Valeron placed the guard's own dagger on the fellow's chest where it covered his heart. Without the slightest compunction, he pushed.

Leaving the dagger in the dead man's chest to arrest the blood flow, Valeron turned him over to face the wall, as though asleep. He might fool someone for a time; this was night, after all, and Valeron needed every second he could steal. Once he'd locked the grille and retrieved Aleysha's dagger, he locked the door of an empty cell and hurled the keys within, with the wad of blood-soaked cloth.

Alert as among hostile foothills, Valeron swung along the corridor. A slavering stooped thing peered out at him from its cubicle; a wrinkled creature with stringy white hair and pendulous, shriveled breasts. It screamed at him as he passed. Though it might have been mercy to run that once-woman through, he went on, walking with knees bent, ready for anything.

Valeron went quickly up the old steps to the big iron door at their tip. He hesitated, took a deep breath, and laid hold of the door handle.

It refused to open.

He pulled, twisted, pushed; the great iron door gave not the tiniest fraction. He glanced over his shoulder; no, there'd be no key to this lock on that ring. This was no jail, but a private prison for very special prisoners. Each guard, once relieved, would lock in his successor. Hissing a coarse oath, Valeron went slowly back down the steps.

Wait?

No; certainly then he must fight his way out, and that might prove impossible. More men would be attracted by the noise, and then more. Resolutely, he set off down the long corridor flanked by iron gratings that doored dirty stone cubicles. Most were empty, the guard's torch showed him. Someone—no, some*thing* gibbered at him from a dark cell. The Branarian goosefleshed without particular compassion for the creature that had been a man; there were occupied cells, too, beneath his keep on Branarius. Some enemies it were better quietly to incarcerate, rather than to make martyrs by doing death on them.

Perhaps such is what Darcus Cannu planned for me . . .

An open cell marked the end of the passage. Raising the torch, he peered within. It was empty even of bunk or straw. Frowning, curious, he went in. Why was there no dust on this patch of floor, while the rest of the cell—

The floor gave way beneath him and Valeron and the torch whooshed into darkness.

SIX

Sword and Tooth

VALERON dropped perhaps twice the length of his body. Behind he heard the treacherous stone scrape and bang back into place; a counterbalanced block of stone that opened onto—a chute!

He smacked painfully onto it, flailing, losing the torch, watching it fly spectacularly through the air while he slid down a steel-smooth surface. He banged his elbow, abraded his skin. At the bottom he slid-rolled and sprawled. Both arms smarted from more than one abrasion, his head roared, and he was disoriented.

With a brief kaleidoscopic burst of sparks the torch struck ground or floor. Darkness closed and he knew the bright lights he saw existed only behind his eyes. He waited, striving to remain conscious and alert. Slowly the dancing lights faded into the darkling murk that surrounded him. His back protested when he sat up, and he cursed it as a traitor. The torch was gone, having dashed itself out against the floor of this—pit? Nor had he means to light it anew. He sat still, waiting with little patience for his eyes to accustom themselves to the dark and report their findings to his spinning brain.

There was little to see and less to report. He was somewhere beneath the dungeons that were beneath the palace. A pit, reached by a trapdoor that closed automatically once the weight that opened it had pitched onto the chute. The secret final disposal of difficult prisoners? Probably.

No glimmer allayed the chthonian dark. No sound disturbed tomblike silence.

"Tomb!" he muttered. "Maybe so—I smell death here."

He felt about behind him with his hands. The gently

45

inclining chute was smooth as polished metal. It had been made by the Ancients! Only they created such; the shipfields were of such a finish, the smoothness, the lack of seam, the polished, gleaming vitrescence of a sword-blade. Elder Saldon had discovered to Valeron that the Ancients had possessed means to heat earth and rock to such unthinkable temperatures as to fuse them into solid sheets of—Saldon called it *trinitite*. Stuff alike the porphyroid rock on Branarius it was, with its igneous crystals of feldspar and quartz, and the shiny basalt of his own keep.

But the name and the How of it mattered not at all. He was in some sort of black hole beneath the palace—how far?

That thought drumming in his brain, he rose, turned, and launched himself up the incline, running—until his boots slipped and he fell to skitter down once more. With a curse, he rose to his haunches. Take off—no, he'd not remove boots in unknown dark! He put back his hand for the comforting feel of the sword-hilt. He wished it were his own weighty, overlong blade rather than the shortish Carmeian glaive; wished that and other things.

Perhaps he could crawl up.

He could and did, coming at last to the chute's top, where it joined a vertical sheet of the same smooth stuff. Carefully he stood, planting his feet so as not to fall, and raised his arms. Outstretched fingers at the ends of straight arms touched nothing. He sighed, peering up into the darkness, trying to gauge his fall, knowing that only a few centimeters beyond reach was the counterbalanced stone that gave into the prison.

All was planned so that none could return from this place: what then awaited him down here?

He trotted down the incline, balancing himself with outstretched arms. Whatever the secret of the unseamed surface, the vertical one behind him assured against scaling.

Then, he thought grimly, *I must find another way*.

With that thought came hope—and something else.

As he started forward into the subterrene blackness, he heard a sound. A scraping, slithering sound, something from the otherworld of necromancy and the awful time of destruction and horror. What else could live, down here? Something ... something that *hissed,* faintly, and made a susurrant sliding sound. Valeron strove to send his 'eyes ahead of him, to pierce a gloom unequaled by the darkest night on his native Branarius.

Eyes stared at him.

No torchlight dimmed the yellow glow of eyes that flamed like golden spots of light somewhere ahead. How far? How large, those eyes that flamed like golden candles? Size and distance were impossible to determine in this gloom. Yet as he watched, his heart thudding, those xanthic eyes rose, and rose—until Valeron's neck was bent; he was looking *up*ward! The eyes blazed at him from a level higher than his head.

His nape proclaimed its presence with a comfortless prickling. Beneath the overtight Carmeian helm, his scalp joined the sensation. Valeron of Branarius had far rather that a half-score men awaited him, with drawn swords, than this unknown set of eyes, without face, without body.

Yellow eyes seemed to look at him and through him, piercing Palatine cuirass and tunic beneath, the hair on his chest and his flesh and bone; the eyes of the unknown seemed to inspect his vitals, his very marrow.

As he carefully repositioned his feet, one struck something with a faint *clonk*. He froze, keeping his gaze fastened on the eyes. They did not flicker. Slowly Valeron sank, buttocks onto heels, and reached out to find the object at his feet.

His fingers ran over a smooth surface, poked into holes, found smaller slits, a gaping, barbed surface. Smooth on top; toothy on the bottom was the thing he touched, and he liked not the shiver it put upon him. He knew what he'd found. Wondering how long it had lain there, how many others lay about in this pit of Kroy, he picked up the human skull and straightened. His eyes had never left those golden others.

He hefted the skull. Unwavering, unblinking eyes stared back at him.

Did they? Could the creature see him? His eyes would not be visible, like the luminous ones he watched; some animals' eyes were noctiluminescent; a human's were not. *I am less visible to* it *than it is to me, with its eyes aglow. But that yields little knowledge; how great is it? How far? Tall, aye, but what bulk?*

He had no way of knowing, and Valeron wished fervently that he wore the gear of an edgeman, not an ornamental guard; a *real* warrior went nowhere without a strike-a-light about him.

How long he stood staring he did not know. The thing ahead neither moved nor made the faintest sound. As if breathing could somehow tell him aught, he strained his ears. He heard nothing. *Some* thing *from the shadow-world of warlocks and daemons, then,* he thought, *some pet of Lord Kroy of the Unending Dark; no breathing creature. Well—a test then*! Swift as the thought he drew back the skull, sighted on the eyes, and threw.

The eyes moved! The skull bounded, partially shattering, from a wall behind the creature and clattered noisily on the floor-stuff. Definitely no more than twice his own length away, the eyes had snapped aside before the missile reached them. How had the owner of those golden eyes known of the silent, rushing approach of the hurled cranium?

The eyes swayed into position again. And stared.

Valeron stared back. It was neither fear nor elation that nibbled at his brain, now, but anger. He'd had enough of this staring match in silent darkness. He drew sword and shouted challenge.

"Ho! What are you, there? Come, charge, Kroy's daemon! I'll spit you for the breakfast I'm missing on your account."

Silence. Silence and the unwavering yellow gaze.

Valeron started to charge, considered; changed his mind. Long ago he had learned not to charge the unknown; learned that he who said "When in doubt, *charge!*" spoke either from false bravado or stupidity. True, it was his motto and his people loved it. But he knew better than to make such advice anything approaching habit.

He hunkered down again to feel about the floor with his left hand until he found a smooth length that felt like an arm bone and then another, probably the unconnected lower half. Rising, he sheathed his sword. Balancing a chunk of bone in either hand, he drew back the left and let fly. Instantly he sent the ulna whizzing after the first bone, throwing to the eyes' right, which was the direction they had taken in dodging.

He hit it, with a loud sound almost metallic.

A hissing, a scrabbling, a bobbing of the eyes, a chopping sound (of great jaws?)—and once again the eyes stared emotionless at him. Valeron railed. He bellowed invective and obscenity and searched his mind for new combinations of words. Then, with sword in hand, he advanced into the dark.

A step he took. Two. Five, six, and the eyes loomed closer, still unmoving; seven—and suddenly the blackness dissolved into the Ancients' bluewhite light. Glowing from the very walls, it made him blink and squint. He halted, startled but unamazed; he had seen the automatic fluorescence of the Ancients afore.

Squinting beneath a hand shading his eyes, he glared.

His companion in the subterrene cavern was a monster reptile, a sea-serpent stranded ashore, a dragon with scintillant scales and fantastic golden eyes that glittered like gems. Gold and silver and topaz!

And what did it *guard*, this great serpent with head and neck rearing some two meters above the floor, nearly touching the pit's ceiling? Behind it stretched its length, perhaps ten meters.

Nor was this a pit, or a room, but a tunnel. Walls and ceiling reflected the light from the polished glassiness of the Ancients' *trinitite*. The floor was littered with bones; skeletons in bits and pieces. Skulls grinned. Scraps of cloth were strewn about. Valeron assumed the creature ate flesh, spat forth bone and cloth. He saw no mail and no weapons.

The guardian of the death-tunnel hissed. Its long jaws gaped, jaws lined with gleaming teeth like the bluish metal of the sword he held—and nigh half the length of its blade. The eyes stared down at him. The creature swayed, swayed, seeming to strain . . . and then Valeron saw its leash. Tension fled him in a great flowing rush and he laughed aloud.

The guardian could not advance. It strained against a slender silver length of cord that was smaller in diameter than Valeron's least finger. With wide-braced feet, he stood and returned its glare with equal ferocity.

"So, great worm! You cannot advance, hey? Yet you guard the way, and I would have passage. How long have you guarded this place, Father of Worms? Judging from the bone-yard, a long time! Since the days of the Ancients, since before the Wrath of Siense and the renascence? How long, Guardian? Why not have a relax and a snooze whilst Valeron passes, eh?"

His voice had no apparent effect on serpent or unblinking eyes. He wondered: could it be deaf? "Here, take this gift as toll." He bent and caught up an ivory tibia and something else of bone and threw them, one after the other. Each the serpent avoided with ease even at this brief distance. Its movements were blurred flashes of silver.

Deaf it might be; blind it was not. Its speed awed the Branarian.

"Not blind, and fast as a loosed arrow." His voice was good, a comfort in this eerie realm of the fearsome, beneath the abode of man. "Hmm . . ."

Valeron car Nadh leaned against the glowing wall to study the reptile and the passageway beyond it. It was leashed here that it might not stray farther, to make its way up into the castle—or what had been builded there when first the creature had been caught and leashed. It dodged his missiles like a harmless coward—but there were the bones. Valeron noticed then: no bones lay behind the guardian.

No one had passed.

He considered. Those others had been tricked or dumped weaponless through the trapdoor. None other had faced old silverscales with a weapon; none lay about, no metal winked from the floor. Only bones littered this comfortless abode of evil and death, this bone yard mouldering beneath the former abode of long-dead men.

Valeron decided; Valeron paced forward.

The great head blurred and the neck rippled and Valeron danced back faster than ever in his life. Toothy jaws snapped shut in front of his face with a frightful clack. In that instant of almost-death and the dodging of it, the Branarian's arm swung like a thing with a mind of its own. The shining blade clanged on the shining serpentine head and slid—*slid, without cutting*—down the narrow pate and into one baleful eye.

The head snapped away without a sound while Valeron fell against the wall, staring, his arm twitching and tingling.

There was no blood, no ichor, no sign of eyeball or wound. Nor had the creature emitted any sound of pain or rage, though one of its eyes was gone. Valeron tried to remember what had happened, fighting the numbing haze in his mind. It had been so fast! Had there been a little bell-like tinkle? A crackle? Had he really seen a faint bluish flash of light and felt a jolt to his arm, as if he had struck his elbow? Or was it his own staggering mind? And the strange odor . . .

The silver-scaled serpent of the pit stared at him, its mouth opening to hiss, and it stared with but one eye. The other was only a dark hole in the side of its head. Valeron's eyes scanned the floor for blood or eyeball—there; something gleamed, twinkled up at him! Carefully, sword ready and eyes on the snake, he squatted and patted the floor to find the tiny twinkling object. He picked it up betwixt thumb and forefinger—and kicked himself backward.

The flattened man-thick head of the serpent or dragon swished past his eyes and again those terrible jaws snapped. Sitting on the tunnel floor, Valeron laughed aloud, laughed to bolster his courage and to shake the reptile's. It straightened sinuously, swaying above him, straining at its silvery leash. The guardian glared at the man in one-eyed silence.

"Uh!" Valeron jerked his hand with an oath and glanced down to find blood on his thumb.

Something had cut him—*a serpent's eye?*

A wave of reaction to the eerie ran up his spine. He squinted at the twinkly thing, shaking it in his palm. It gleamed, sparkled, and through it he could see his sweaty hand. It was a gleaming bit of . . . quartz? Plast? It resembled the viewscreens on the shuttle-ships!

Slowly he raised his head to stare at the serpent.

"So," he said, and he whispered, more awed than relieved, for now the guardian was even more a representative of the unknown than before. "So. Not the grandfather of all snakes ... you're a minion of Siense, a *creation* of the Ancients. Made, *made* like their ships, and set here to guard their secrets against any who came after the Wrath! What dark secrets lie behind you, snake—beneath Carmeis City? Well then—come you here with that other eye!"

Again he raised sword and stepped deliberately forward—and slipped and staggered on a rolling bit of bone. He fell.

He flung himself sidewise so that the lashing muzzle crashed into his chest, a centimeter out of reach of the teeth as they clashed. Valeron was slammed backward the length of his body, to roll across the floor among chittering bones. He got slowly to his feet, and this time his epithets were for himself. Shivering and cursing he stood, and slowly he ceased, and grinned.

"Well, silverscales, I was stupid and you nearly added more to your bone collection, eh?"

Then swiftly, Valeron bent and snatched up a bone and threw it and another and a handful and hurled them and he found a skull and heaved that too at the weaving, dodging head with its one yellow eye and its empty socket, and then he ran. Straight down the passage he raced, hugging the wall opposite the serpent. Skidding to a stop, he banged back and shoulders against the wall as he raised the sword with both hands.

None too soon, that; mouth agape, the head came flashing down at him. Even while it started its lunge, its prey was dodging leftward, swinging his steel blade. The outsize teeth clicked shut, taking away a morsel of flesh as they slid off the tense-thewed side of his thigh. At the same time, the sword's edge crashed into the blind side of the creature's head. With a clang, the brand slid off scales of metal or that other stuff—plast, perhaps.

The neck arched and reared—and Valeron rode with it, hanging on with one brawny arm wrapped around a neck thick as his body at the ribs.

The metal serpent hissed its metal hiss and shook its metal head while it arched its metal neck. Valeron let go so as to drop down under the head, close in to the body where the guardian's tether held it in semi-check. Here the man was harder to reach; the head must needs curve under its own neck to seize him. There was time for the drawing of his right arm far back, the cranking of his elbow high into the air.

As the serpent sought awkwardly to double its thick neck to strike beneath itself, Valeron lunged, rather than struck, attacking in what other ages had called a *passado*, a powerful driving stab following the rapid advance of one leg. He went to one knee with the force of his thrust—and felt the terrible jolt up his arm again as the sword entered the reptile's eye. There was a tinkling, a flash of blue, and, instantly, an acrid odor.

Then the blind, lashing head struck him in the guts and he went over backward, falling against the serpentine belly, retching. His fingers flexed open and the sword dropped. While an ocean of ink seemed flowing over him, sucking him into unconsciousness, he saw the neck slumping down and knew that even a blind monster would find him easy prey now.

SEVEN

Science and Superstition

VALERON car Nadh came to his senses with an ache in his intestines where the metal-plated head had struck, and a matching ache in his lungs. He struggled, realized a great weight lay on his chest, and opened his eyes. He saw a gleaming ceiling lit by the pale azure light of the Ancients. An attempt to move told him that his body and one arm were pinned, heavily. Lying thus weighted on his back, he lifted his head as much as possible.

He lay beneath the inert body of the guardian.

But if it is a machine created by the Ancients, he mused, *how can it die?* A shakingly horrible thought followed: *Can the ships die?*

Could it be that his smashing the thing's "eyes" had ended its artificial life? This he decided was true—and . . . if one smashed the viewscreens of the big shuttle-ships, would the craft become inoperable? That, he thought, would be a crime worse than slaying an emperor. But he filed the information away in his brain lest ever he need it . . .

Wriggling, straining, he got one arm free of the reptile's dead weight. He waved the arm to restore circulation before placing both hands against the body of the guardian. Valeron shoved. He strained. Slowly, he slid from beneath it, though not before the metal scales had torn tunic and underlying flesh. Once he'd struggled free, he lay still, gasping, until his breath came again steadily.

Then he got to his feet and looked down at the guardian.

Machine or no, he felt something resembling pity, regard; for untold ages the artificial reptile had abided here, tethered fast, guardian of something the Ancients wished guarded. Now, among the bones marking its long success, it was dead.

A creation of the Ancients! What had those men not been able to do!

While he regained strength and full use of his body, Valeron pondered their accomplishments. No man understood the use of the ships in which they traveled among the seven worlds; ships devised by the Ancients, centuries ago. The soft light from the globes never ceased to illumine, nor even flickered; how long had they burned coldly, fed by some magic of the Ancients and their relationship with Siense before his Wrath destroyed them? Six of the seven worlds, Saldon said, were artificial or at least had been hung artificially, like ornaments in space. Long centuries ago they had been dragged across space by ships far larger than the intrasystem shuttle craft that were all that remained. The planets had been urged into orbit about a sun called Carmen, followed by a string of meaningless numbers and letters in the Old Style. The complex was called the Carmen System. Each world was known to be equidistant from its neighbor; each world was approximately equidistant from the sun. Distance was measured in travel-time aboard the shuttlers that were bound by their controls to the worlds of this system. No one knew how far was the sun; none wished to find out.

The symbolic designation of the empire consisted of six large pearls, connected by chains, all connected by more links of chain like spokes to the center pearl, Carmeis. And so it was. Carmeis revolved about the sun (so it was said, though visual evidence was precisely to the contrary); the other worlds revolved about Carmeis. Saldon was sure there were uncounted and uncounted other worlds; each winking light in the night sky was another sun.

The shuttle-ship control panels contained but seven destination buttons. The ships could not leave this system. Nor would there be tampering with controls, until and unless future Saldons somehow divined the mechanism of those ships.

And the Ancients had made this creature, too! Without limit had been their knowledge, Valeron thought in some awe, gazing upon the dead guardian. But that was why Siense destroyed them and their civilization in his o'erchallenged Wrath.

With a shrug of barbarian insouciance, Valeron returned to what was important; he picked up his sword. He walked past the reptile into the depths of the tunnel. Above him was a ceil of the shiny Ancient-stuff; on either side of him the wall was composed of the same material. This cavern had doubtless been here and the geniuses of long ago had widened it, shored it up, and smoothed its walls and ceiling made steel-hard by ... whatever method they used. A process similar to the making of glass, it was thought, but using a heat so intense as to be inconceivable.

Valeron stopped. He stared, scalp prickling.

The wall to his left was suddenly no longer opaque.

He was looking into a vast room full of gleaming banks of controls and viewscreens, console after console of controls for ... something. Starting forward, he discovered that the wall was still there; it was translucent plast, like the snake's eyes and the ships' screens. A fortune was here, in plast! He raised a fist and struck it a blow that hurt even while it resounded, gonglike, along the tunnel. No man living could make aught like this!

Marveling, Valeron walked along the wall until he came to a door of the same stuff. He studied the fourteen characters printed on it in the alphabet now modified by the centuries, so that Velquen's name was spelled with six letters, among other changes. The Branarian shrugged, uncomprehending, at the letters C E N T R A L   C O N T R O L and pushed open the door to enter the room.

Chaos! Noise struck like a palpable force.

Amid the humming and steady chatter of machinery, he felt a vibration akin to that aboard the ships. Hurriedly he backed out, heart pounding. The door swung shut with a hiss—and noise and vibration ceased instantly. Valeron stood still, marveling at more Ancient-magic.

The urge to push open the door was irresistible. Again there was sound, chatter, vibration; again it ended once the door had sighed shut. Valeron took a deep breath, and walked into the noise beyond the door of Central Control.

The room was vast. It was filled with long lines of silver-blue cabinets, separated by aisleways. Every cabinet was pocked with little round insets with white faces that bore numerals and tiny red pointers that quivered beneath the quartz-like stuff he knew was "glast," re-invented on Sid-Alors a half-century ago. There were squares, too, of the same, and oblongs, and ovals. Everywhere were the things of the ships, which Saldon called "dials." They were interspersed with panels and banks of buttons, and levers and wheels.

Here was much wealth; so much plast in many forms and several colors would make coins enough to double those in use on Branarius.

Pulling a handle in one console, he opened a door to peer within at weird, living, blue flame. Valeron slammed the door hurriedly.

When he rounded a bank of blue metal housing a thirty meter length of dials and buttons and levers, he came upon a pile of bones. Valeron stared down. Once this had been a man—one of the Ancients!

He bent to touch a bone, watched it turn to ashy dust under his fingers. Those crumbled scraps had once been this man's clothes. Amid crumbling bone and fabric lay bits of plast and metal: a buckle, some completely unrecognizable items, a little cylinder whose purpose eluded Valeron car Nadh. A rectangular bit of metal sprouted a pin from its back and a little sheet of plast across its face. Beneath the plast were the old characters: KABIR, JAGADIS R. And beneath that: CHIEF ENGINEER.

Valeron dropped it and dusted his hands; he did not rob the dead. "Jewelry. Hmp. Looks like any other skeleton, too."

Yet awe was with him as he stood amid humming, churning, chattering machinery all around. The room was of more vastness than the imperial throne-room. What had happened, so long ago, to KABIR, JAGADIS R. CHIEF ENGINEER? What had been his life, his purpose here? Or . . . was that a name? Per-

haps they were ward-words and Valeron would do well
to appropriate the ancient pin. He squinted at the
squiggles that apparently identified (?) the endless
bands of instruments and dials in their gleaming metal
bins:

LIGHTS: East Sector. LIGHTS: West Sector.
LIGHTS: North Sector. LIGHTS: South Sector. AIR-
CON: East Sector . . . and on, and on. Tentatively he
put out a barbarian finger to touch a black button incused with a white "O," beneath a plate reading
LIGHTS: Central—whatever that was. He touched it
gingerly; it yielded. He jerked back as the button gave
with a click, and the panel's light went out. The whining hum descended the scale—to cease. In horror he
stared, then looked desperately about him. Beside the
button, another was marked "I," and he nerved himself
to push it, in hopes of rectifying whatever awful thing
he might have done.

The light on the little panel winked on. Within, a dial
crept up its line of numbers and something within the
gleaming blue cabinet hissed and began to hum anew.

Valeron car Nadh resolved to touch nothing else. He
passed on along the line of cabinets with their dials and
bluish lights, their buttons and wheels and other controls. Past a black cylinder on the floor he moved, a
small black cylinder with which Chief Engineer Jagadis
R. Kabir had anciently sought to protect himself from
another such cylinder. But that identical black tube of
lesser deadliness had drilled a hissing, instantly cauter-
ized hole through his chest, in the darkling reaches of
yesterdays forgotten and misunderstood.

Here, Valeron resolved, he would return with Saldon
and other Elders . . . *if ever I find a way out!*

Passing along another metal-floored aisle between
control-studded metal cabinets, he returned to the door,
and the tunnel. Outside, he paused a moment, looking
reflectively back at the Pandora's Box that had ended
the civilization of humankind here and given way to
dark savagery and a misty, tenuous new upward creep-
ing toward sanity and a new civilization.

Staring at the Machines of the jealous god Siense, the
Branarian shuddered. Valeron shuddered, as never he

had at man or beast or odds, or the crashing and howl-
ing of Nature in its frightful lashing across Branarius.

For those were known things.

This was magic.

Then Valeron car Nadh walked on into the cavern,
leaving behind the bright-lit Central Control chamber;
the metal-scaled serpent; Kabir, Jagadis R.; and the
little black cylinder of death that barbarian eyes had
seen and ignored.

He had but one interest, now: a way out.

No idea was with him as to how long he'd been down
here, how long he'd lain unconscious, how long he'd
been held in thrall by the power room's fascination.
Now he hurried, striding along the blue-lit corridor
beneath the Imperial Palace.

And he came to its end. "Damnèd be!"

This sudden blocking of the cavern was not human-
made, unless it had come about through the mighty ex-
plosives of the Ancients. The tunnel was closed by a
mass of rock and earth, obviously fallen. Fending
against despair, Valeron stood looking at the impass-
able barrier. There had been another entry/exit then—
and it was no more. At some time in the mists of the
pasts, tons of granite and dirt had crashed down to seal
it. Nor would there be any fossicking his way out, as
there was no way of knowing for how many centimeters
or meters the pile of torn mountain lay in the passage.

Mayhap they did this blockage on it deliberately.

Perhaps the barbarism that had followed the Wrath
had been foreseen. The other ingress they had left
open, concealed—and barred, not with a door or a sign,
but with a creature to shake the minds of men more
dominated by superstition than possessed of knowledge.
Yet they had left the machinery running . . . or perhaps
they had not. Perhaps Kabir, Jagadis had been slain as
he was on the point of stopping all activity in that vast
hall of metal and plast and glast?

Does it matter? Valeron questioned himself as he
turned and paced determinedly back along the soft-lit
corridor.

Am I trapped here? Would he share this tomb with
Kabir and the argent serpent and the scattered bones of

past intruders? Had Valeron of Branarius come so igno-
miniously and senselessly to the end of his—

No!

Here; he had passed it afore. A vertical line marked
the wall; a seam! He stepped hurriedly to it, ran his fingers along the crack˙ that ran with mathematical
straightness from floor to ceiling—an artifical crack. A
door?

The Branarian explored. The usual eighty-five centimeters to the crack's left was: nothing.

How could this be a door when there were no hinges,
no sign of its back edge or of a broken-off handle?

He pushed. He leaned against it, pushed with all his
might until the corded muscles of his calves bunched
like aliani under the skin, biceps straining at the fabric
of the Carmeian tunic, back swelling and bulging with
effort. His feet slipped on the floor's smooth surface; he
nearly fell; the wall gave no notice of his strength. Stepping back, he drew sword and poked at the crack. His
teeth dented his lower lip. The crack proved too tiny to
admit more than a millimeter of sword-point. He
waggled it but stopped at once; there was no give. Valeron knew that to persist would succeed only in snapping off his weapon's point.

Stepping back with a sigh, he stared at the tiny crack.
Surely it indicated a doorway.

Bafflement was with him, that and a barbarian's anger at the inscrutable and immovable. He smote the
wall with the sword to produce a clicking, clanking
sound and a spark of metal off metal. Not the tiniest
shardlet of the Ancient-stuff chipped away.

Standing there in the cavern that, even in the soft
azure light, had begun to seem a tomb again, Nadh's
son of Branarius considered Gray-green eyes glowered
at the tantalizing crack in the impregnable wall. He
paced to his left a meter and more; back to his right
twice that distance. No other marking broke the
smoothness of the wall, nor the floor.

There was no way out. If there were indeed a door
here, there was no means of opening it.

"Branar do damnation on them!"

For no rational reason he wheeled, cursing, to glare

at the wall behind him, across the corridor from the crack. His curses and obscenities rang hollowly back at him from the long-deserted corridor, echoing and echoing again. Then they faded from his lips; with a frown, he stepped close.

The wall's smoothness was broken by a rectangular patch no larger than his palm. It was a patch of glast, or a niche covered with the stuff. Valeron squinted at it, trying to pierce its cloudy not-quite translucence. Slowly he raised hand to touch it.

The noise behind him spun him around before he'd touched the wall plate. A high-pitched whine reminded of the sound of a shuttle-ship's opening its doors. Aye, and the crack was wider! He leaped to it, poked in his fingers, dropped sword to shove eight fingers into the crevice and lean his weight against it, straining. There was no yielding.

Withdrawing his fingers with a curse, he took two leftward steps, reinserted his hands, and pulled in that direction—with the same lack of result.

Slowly he relaxed his straining sinews. Slowly he turned his eyes back on the little plate of glast on the wall opposite. It was alive! A saffron light flickered behind the glast—mocking him? A low growl rose up from his throat and he sprang back across the corridor to jam his hand against the panel.

Behind him, the wall opened as though the panel were triggered by the mere presence of his hand to send some mechanical command to a mechanical brain that triggered in turn a relay—that set in motion the ages-old machinery.

A section of the wall slid back into its slot to reveal a doorway of more than a meter's width.

His hand still covering the plate, leaning against it, Valeron stared over his shoulder at the magically widening gap in the wall. He grinned.

Pouncing like a cat intent on crafty prey, the War-lord of Branarius leaped across the tunnel and, sword before him, into the little room behind the door.

The room was tiny, just over a meter deep. Before him was a blank wall; to his left another; behind him the open door and the cavern. The wall on his right was not quite blank; it contained a black rectangle of metal. Three buttons protruded from its surface, one above the other. Each was incused with a single character: "D," and "B," and "I."

Valeron hesitated, nearly overwhelmed by the mocking unknown. His heart pounded.

As he hesitated, the door trundled back to slip into position again, sealing him off from the cavern. Just as it started to close, the cavern's lights went out. They did not dim, or flicker, or waver; they were suddenly just *not*, with blackness where there had been light. At the same instant, the walls of the tiny room around him assumed the warm blue glow of the Ancients' incomprehensible light.

Once again Valeron stood in shocked awe of the unknown. Ever had men feared the power of Siense above that of all gods, or of necromancy or death; all that took place here occurred with no visible controlling agency, happened through the hands of men long dead. Valeron car Nadh knew that he was in the realm of Siense, in his very keep.

The Warlord of Branarius touched his forehead.

Here was magic. Magic the likes of which the shaman-priests of the Sungoli with their genuine powers of mind had never dreamed, much less performed. Driving rain, crashing thunder, forked tongues of blue-white lightning; avalanches, landslides, snowstorms; tornadoes and the rumbling horror of earthquakes; the charges of maddened beasts and maddened men; all these things Valeron had witnessed, or experienced. Nor had he known fear worth the mentioning.

In this black-then-bluelit-then-black-again pit beneath the palace of Empire he had felt its prickly touch more than once. And now he knew it again, felt its chill hand clutching at the still-sore muscles of his lower abdomen where the head of the metal serpent had butted him.

With effort, Valeron shook it off.

He took a deep breath and stabbed a finger at the first button.

The baffled man laughed aloud, for the whining sound began anew. Back slid the wall, and the lights ceased to glow in the cubicle—but returned in the tunnel. Laughing a bit too heartily, Valeron stepped forward for another glance out into the marvelous place he has first thought of as a pit, a tomb. Then he stood tall and straight within the cubicle, and addressed himself to the door.

"I, Valeron Barbaros car Nadh called Mighty, Warlord of Branarius, command you to *close*," he said—and chuckled like a boy when the door commenced to slide back into position, even before he had finished his grandiose command.

He waited only long enough for the gentle azurite light to return to the tiny chamber. Then Valeron pushed the second button: "B."

Nothing happened.

The Branarian waited a long moment, frowning, wondering. *The first opes the door; how is it that the second accomplishes naught?* Boyish jubilation faded, and nervousness grew. But his hand went out, a trifle tentatively—and pushed the third button.

Gray eyes flashed about, wide and fearful with a barbarian's natural dread and awe of the unseen and incomprehensible. Amid a whirring sound, a sensation of movement . . . he felt it in his belly, and his knees bent. Gods! What witchery was this? *Was* he moving? The sensation he felt in legs and stomach—was it . . . could this be . . . *upward motion?*

Valeron Nadh's son could think and write his name and count to a hundred. Though he understood the method of counting further, necessity had never been with him. He feared neither man nor beast and had been known to scoff at the gods. Not now. Now his heart pounded and his eyes rolled in atavistic, unreasoning horror and dark apprehension. He sent a mental prayer to Siense and to Branar and Lady Aria too, and even Sente. The old ward-words of the Sungoli rose in the mind of the man who had been Sanxarkhl of the Sungoli: *Wraiths of our fathers, smile on our efforts, frown on our enemies, and above all and else protect us from the fearsome powers of the Dark One!*

Someone answered him in his haunted loneliness and icy apprehension.

Whether prayer or the Sungoli invocation or more magic of the Ancients, *something* brought the sensation of motion to a stomach-lurching halt. He gasped. His legs remained bent warily and his hand fisted around sword-pummel. *Had* he been borne somehow upward? A swift glance about discovered no change in his surroundings. The little metal cubicle remained but that. Through that door, surely then, was the somber cavern, the mysterious door marked CENTRAL CONTROL, and the bones . . .

Or were they there? Were they now . . . *somewhere below?*

Still Valeron stood, half-crouching, feet apart, sword ready. He longed for his own mail and a buckler on his left arm, which felt naked. His eyes snapped glances about, wide now and animal-gleaming. His searching gaze fastened on the plate set in the wall, and its three buttons. He stared at them. What had he done? Now nervousness was with him at pushing one of them again—the second one again?

No! He chose the known over the leering unknown.

The Warlord of Branarius raised a hesitant finger to the button marked "D." He faced the door with sword up and ready, waiting, waiting for . . . what?

Slowly, the door began to slide back.

EIGHT

Barbarian and Slave

As the door moved with its high-pitched whine of some hidden mechanism, there was the heavy rustle of cloth on its other side. Valeron's teeth gritted.

Then the door was open. Valeron was looking into a brightly-lit room, a stone-walled chamber whose walls were hung with violet drapings. A great shield with sword and ax beneath it gleamed on one wall high above a trefoil-arched window that admitted the bright light of day. A big wooden desk was backed by a chair covered in leather. Along a wall lounged a divan covered with purfled amethystine cloth from whose borders dangled gold tassels.

The room also contained a man.

He was staring at Valeron, his eyes wide with shock and perhaps fear as he looked upon an apparent guardsman—dirty, and in torn cloak. The other wore the cerulean blue of the Palatine Guard and the silvery casque with its nodding crest of uss feathers dyed sea-green; his cloak was white. The guardsman stood near the desk. Open-mouthed, he stared at the gaping wall and the big man within its niche.

His mouth closed; his brows descended as he gained some control of himself. "How in Kroy's name did ... who are you. Guardsman, and how came you here— and *filthy*, at that?"

Since he wore the same uniform, Valeron decided to adopt a straightforward air. "I encountered some trouble and had to earn my pay, for once. There are other uniforms—but as to that other question—what are *you* doing here?"

Valeron recognized the desk and the lambrequin hanging at the window, the newly created coat-of-arms.

The escutcheon had been created by Emperor Velquen for his trusted and valued prime minister. Valeron had seen it afore; this was Darcus Cannu's office in the palace.

The other man's frown deepened. He was still wavering, with shock on him, but of one thing he was certain, and he made it plain: "You don't talk that way to your vice-prefect, fellow. You know well who I am. But that *door*—"

The wall was starting to close. Evidently it remained open long enough for the . . . occupant?—passengers?—of the little room to depart, ere it closed itself. On the point of pushing "D" again, Valeron heard a gasp, from a throat other than the vice-perfect's. As the door slid shut, he saw the sound's source: naked of torso she was, and wearing the brass armband of Carmeian slavery. The seagreen bracelet on her left wrist marked her as a servant of the imperial family.

Valeron halted his hand. He allowed the door to shut off his view. It clicked into position. He waited. Waited, listening, and heard nothing. Remembering that the closing of the doors somehow closed off sound, he waited . . .

Still longer he was moveless, in tactical patience to allow the other man time to approach and start to examine the enchanted wall. The tip of Valeron's finger again depressed the first button, and he steeled himself for a leaping charge. He was sure that Prefect Alerku's adjutant Shanaru was an intelligent fighting man, not appointed for political reasons. Valeron was prepared.

Back slid the wall. From less than a meter away, the vice-prefect of the Palatine Guard stared again at the man in the uniform of his own command. Stared at him—and at the upward-whipping sword as the big man lunged from the secret room.

Valeron was right about Shanaru. As the other man lunged, the Carmeian proved his competence. A sidewise wrench of his body avoided the gleaming death in Valeron's hand. At the same time Shanaru yanked out his own glaive to parry the vicious backswipe at his head. Neither man wore a buckler; both were cuirassed.

"You asked my name," Valeron said, fixing Shanaru

with a slit-eyed gaze. "And I put the question on you—impolitely. I am Valeron of Branarius."

Across the room the girl gasped again and Valeron glanced at her as she raised dusky knuckles to purple lips.

"*Valeron!*" Shanaru whispered. "Recognition was not with me, and you under that helmet and in our uniform, barbarian. How you came here or came by that uniform is without matter, now—surely our purposes are served just as well by my killing you—before a witness—in the act of escaping!" And he lunged.

Though it was hardly normal or favored, Valeron had fought without buckler before. He beat the other man's sword aside with two hard raps of his own blade and jerked its point back to flick at Shanaru's throat. The Carmeian barely skipped back in time to save his jugular—and his eyes held new respect for his opponent. Behind Valeron the wall section slid shut.

"Girl!" Shanaru called, backing warily. "To the door—call my men!"

Then he was forced to whip his sword up in an attempt to meet Valeron's swift high cut. Again steel rang on steel, and Valeron grunted at the impact. From the edge of his eye, he saw the slave take a frowning step—and halt! She backed against the desk. When she glanced at the door, Valeron prepared to leap to intercept her—but Shanaru renewed attack with a savagery that forced the Branarian to concentrate all his attention on the flickering sliver of Carmeian steel that thirsted for his life.

Peripheral vision showed him the girl running to the door, and he began to consider a retreat to the room-that-moved.

The slave grasped the door's brass handle—and slammed it.

"Girl! *Slave!*" The vice-prefect's voice was a snarl. "I bade you call guards, not close the door! Quickly—"

As he spoke, the Palatine made the error of twitching his eyes in her direction. That sort of error was deadly when one faced a master edgeman whose own eyes watched his opponent's. It was deadly to Vice-Prefect Shanaru. His eyes as they snapped back to his assailant went wide, and wider, and shocked, and then glassy as forty centimeters of Carmeian steel drove through his ornamental cuirass and tunic, into flesh and heart. His sword dropped from fingers that quivered epileptically.

Shanaru slipped down to his knees. Glazing eyes remained fixed on Valeron, while the Palatine's mouth opened to shout. The shout emerged as no more than a bubbling gasp. Giving his sword a twist, Valeron pulled it free and stepped back a pace to avoid Shanaru; the Carmeian pitched forward on his face.

"Considerate," Valeron grunted, "of the emperor to place his coat-of-arms directly over his guardsmen's hearts—as a target!" He turned deep green-gray slits of eyes toward the slave.

She was short, full-bosomed, tawny, with shir-darkened eyes and hair dark as shir spilling loosely down over her dusky shoulders. Her eyes lifted from Shanaru to Valeron. They were so dark as to appear black, those large eyes.

She smiled. "My lord Valeron: I am Jheru, personal servant to the prin—to the empress."

She made him a bow that caused her navel to close like a day-flower while her breasts swung down to dip their dyed tips. Her words were proper, her little bow; why then was feeling with him that she somehow mocked?

"Jheru!" Deliberately he let his eyes roam her, down from heart-shaped face to round, thrusting breasts with purpled crests, returning at leisure to large nigh-black eyes. Beneath the arch of thick black brows, she was staring unabashedly back at him. "I remember you, Jheru. You have changed in six years; you are about her age, as I remember. You've plumped, too," he said, with a grin at the navel that was a smoky cave in tawny belly that was not concave.

"My *lord*," she said, in full command of herself, as a woman chides a boy for a minor misdemeanor.

Slave this one was, he saw, but not in her mind; she bobbed her head at the body at his feet.

"May I suggest you return attention to Her Eminence's late Vice-Prefect of Palatines ... we cannot very well leave him lying here, nor dare we remain long in this place. Shanaru's cloak will cover the rents in your tunic—and *most* of the dirt."

Valeron flashed her his not-handsome wolf's grin and glanced down at Shanaru. A widening spread of burgundy was seeping from beneath the body to stain Darcus Cannu's purple carpet. Teeth in lip, Valeron glanced back at the wall through which he'd come. With impressive lack of distaste, Jheru was removing Shanaru's cloak.

The rustle on its opening, he saw, had been a heavy drape that had hung just beside the hidden doorway. The seam was invisible now even to him who knew it was there; the wall was partially paneled with rich-grained, cinnamon-colored wood—to conceal the door. Valeron snarled a curse. Somewhere behind that damned paneling was a tiny plate to— He sprang forward to sweep back purple drapes. He revealed a bare wall of igneous porphyry, with twinkling crystals of quartz and bright feldspar—and an unusually squarish patch. A few hours ago Valeron would not have noticed it. The plate was well disguised, set rather high on the wall. He clapped a hand over it.

From behind him he heard Jheru's quick intake of breath; the wall scraped, paneling and all, and slid back. Only after it was opening did he hear the whining sound that was now familiar.

"Come here, Jheru. Hold your hand over this spot."

She came, swaying and bouncing with all her body bare above the naval and most of her legs in evidence as well. She lifted a dusky round arm to stretch palm and fingers over the disguised plate while she peered wonderingly into the unnatural recess in the wall.

Grasping Shanaru's body under its arms, Valeron hauled it into the cubicle. He bent Shanaru's legs a little so that the body fit into the room-that-moved. Returning for the dead man's sword, Valeron tossed it in with the body. Unhappily he gazed at the pool of blood on the carpet. He glanced at the girl. No, there was no using what clothing she wore; aside from lacy leather sandals gaiter-strapped up her calfy legs and the slave-let on her arm, she wore naught but a pale yellow-green kirtle, slung low beneath her navel and pushing into the full-fleshed hips that held it up. It fell to a few inches above her knees.

The Branarian grinned; he had a sudden vision of his mopping up the gore with that applegreen kirtle while she stood unhappily by, bare as the day she was born—with a few fascinating differences here and there.

As he'd now have Shanaru's cloak, Valeron used the soiled remnants of his own to mop up the man's thickening blood.

"Must I hold my hand here?"

He glanced up. Jheru was short, and she stretched nearly on tiptoe to reach the plate set high that it might not be noticed—and had not, apparently, through the mists of pasts. Valeron enjoyed the effect of her upstretched arm on her body.

He said "No," and she dropped her arm with a sigh.

Watching him, she rubbed the arm—and jumped with a little squeak when the wall slid back into place.

"Tell me why you came here, and tell me where Darcus Cannu is," he said while he rubbed at the strain with a ruined white cloak.

"I came on her orders, to fetch your sword. Shanaru must have followed—he wanted to play. I was . . . disputing that, when . . . the wall opened. How—"

"I was in the dungeon, and I escaped," he said, without waiting for her question. "Darcus?"

"At the coronation. It was delayed—there was a terrible scare this morning. You didn't know? Just a short time ago."

"A short time ago I was very busy trying to get out of . . . a trap of the Ancients. Carmeis City could have been frightened away—what happened?"

"All the lights went off! Right in the center of the city—the *Ancient* lights! They've *never* failed afore. Fear was with us, but then the lights returned, and many muttered. The priests consulted the gods. Some feared an evil omen and muttered that the gods frowned on the coronation, so soon after the emperor's death."

Valeron snorted. "The gods!" he said, knowing with shocked certainty what had befallen the lights—and who had extinguished them in barbarian ignorance.

"Obviously their displeasure was brief ... Then the ceremony is not over?"

She shook her head. "Barely begun, my lord. Please hurry—we must get out of here, both of us." ·

"This is about the best I can do with the carpet—let us hope Darcus overlooks this spot." He added darkly, "For a while," as he went to the wall-plate and, on the door's opening once more, tossed the blood-smeared cloak in onto Shanaru.

After a moment of thought, Valeron pushed the button marked "B" and sprang back out of the cubicle. The door closed. He assumed that Vice-Prefect Shanaru was on his way down ...

"You said my sword?" He swung the dead man's cloak about himself; clasped it.

She bobbed her head and he watched her most interesting movements while she hurried with short, swift steps across the room to the desk. *No wonder Shanaru wanted to play! And those swollen-calf legs; hesitation would be with me to run race with her! But Oh, the muscles in them ...*

Slaves were made to remain bare above the waist here, he knew, on the theory that it reminded them of their place: their near-nakedness robbed them of self-respect and made them more vulnerable and thus docile. All things, Valeron mused, did not always work out as planned. ·

She bent—sending his eyebrows up—and rose to turn with belt and scabbard sprouting a fluted black pommel. "I left it here when Shanaru—"

She broke off and lifted her thick black brows as he strode to her, his eyes alight as a boy's. Grasping the pommel, he pulled the sword from the sheath she held and slashed it through the air with a wicked *whup-whup!* sound. After a moment of consideration, he took belt and scabbard from her and detached the long sheath. Removing the Carmeian sword-belt, he fastened his own outsize sheath to his own thick black belt with its flashing studs of brass. His sword, Jimarah, he sheathed at his side, then, and Jheru put the other harness and blade back where Darcus Cannu had kept them. His overlong blade—concealed by Shanaru's voluminous cloak—had work to do.

"Now, Jheru. I am to wait in her chamber for the pr—the empress. I shall escort you there. We'll look as if we're exchanging pleasantries; setting a tryst."

Her voice was low and throaty: "That would be nice."

Her remark gained her a slap on the rump from the barbarian outworlder.

Startled but silent, she accompanied him to the door. There he paused for a last glance around—and she seized his wrist to drag him back into the room.

"Your hair! It dangles below the helmet behind, my lord. You may think you have disguise with you, but none behind you will be fooled!"

He made a rueful face and pulled off the already-tight Carmeian casque.

"We must cut your hair," she began, and squeaked when his hand closed on her forearm. Fingers like powerful serpents wrapped around to overlap his thumb past the joint.

"*Cut my hair?* Oh no, little slave, oh no! When there's time with us I will explain about Branarius and our Warrior's Knot. Meanwhile—we must tuck it up under this damned tight helmet."

She smiled at his pronunciation of the ancient oathword; he said it in outworld fashion, in two syllables. The barbarian's mass of long purple-red hair was drawn back, she saw, encircled at his nape with a bit of metal that had been blessed in the temple of the patron goddess of Branarius, the great Mother, Aria. From there it hung loosely halfway down his back—a very broad back, Jheru observed. She helped, behind him on tiptoe, to tuck the swatch of hair up under the outcurving neck-guard of the helmet.

"It is not so—coarse as I'd expected," she said, and bit her lip. Then she inspected, nodded approval of his disguise, and hurried to the door. She peered out into the corridor; reached back a hand. "Come. There is no one."

They emerged from Darcus Cannu's office into a long hallway of pearl-and-chalky stone, lined with tall doors of wood with carven panels and large, squared brass handles above keyholes tall as a man's thumb. Valeron strolled along at the young woman's side. He held back legs wont to move in great strides, striving the while to appear nonchalant and at home in this uniform, in this place.

Her hand in his, they reached the steps at the end of the hall and ascended to the second floor.

A door popped open down the corridor and a woman in her twenties emerged carrying an unladen salver. Her hips were circled by the same green almost-skirt that Jheru wore; her arms and wrists banded by the same slavemarks. She walked rapidly toward them, bare breasts abobbing, and smiled at Jheru. A hazel-eyed look she sent at Valeron, who puffed his chest; the young woman at his side made a sound like a hiss and fingernailed his palm. They walked on in silence. Now a head appeared at the very end of the long corridor, and shoulders, and the body of a boy. A page in the apple-green livery of the palace, he reached the top of the stairs and walked toward them with quick steps. Jheru, on Valeron's left, squeezed his wrist when his other hand started to move across his stomach for the ebony shank of his sword. He desisted; the page drew abreast.

"Is the coronation over yet?" Jheru asked, and the boy paused with a smile.

"Over? No no—now the nobles are swearing fealty to Her Eminence. They'll be slobbering over her sigil for an hour yet. Plenty of time's with you and your friend for . . . whatever you have in mind." His smile broadened. Tossing a hand in a silly wave, he went on past.

Valeron was hard put to refrain from turning. He'd had no experience as spy, walking in disguise among the enemy.

No, they are not the enemy, he reminded himself. *Not all. But—how can I know which are loyal to Aleysha and Empire, and which to Darcus Cannu?*

Jheru stopped and took hold of Valeron's other hand, bringing him to a halt. Having stepped in front of him, she looked up at his face in the manner of a woman at work awinning a man.

"The guard has changed, my lord," she said in a low voice, without moving her lips. "I feared as much."

"What guard? Feared?"

"*Shh!* A sentry stands across from the pr—Her Eminence's door at all hours, night and day. There, look but once and then at me again. There is a niche in the wall across from her door."

He looked over her head—which was easy; he could have planted his chin on her crown with little strain—and saw the indented rectangle in the wall. A pair of booted feet protruded at its base. Beside the niche burned a new flambeau, unnecessary, but traditional in the palace.

"See him? When the new guard comes, he brings a new torch. The other we might have passed; he has a . . . certain interest in . . . Her Eminence's servant." She smiled and tapped her chest, a shiny patch of lighter tan between her breasts. "But this fellow—he has interest only in Darcus Cannu, and a promotion. No man enters those rooms. No man, and you must not."

"We could rid the world of one more of the prime minister's hirelings . . ."

"My lord, curb your ferocity," she said, and warm hands squeezed his. "The slightest noise will bring more. No, I shall go in. Do you turn your head toward me as you pass him, and go on down the steps and out of the palace."

"And how in Kroy's name am I to enter, girl?"

She lifted one deeply tan shoulder on a shrug that brought a delightful movement to her chest, movement that he could not avoid watching and enjoying. With difficulty he lifted his eyes to her face.

"My name is Jheru," she said, a chiding. "The gardens, my lord . . . perhaps a window . . ."

Then she turned and, leaving one hand in his, walked on. When they were between the sentry and the door, she stepped away from Valeron. Smiling in reluctant parting, for the guard's benefit, she stretched her arm to its fullest reach before she released his fingers.

"Until later then, love," she said, and her voice was the musical note of the snowy uss birds at mating-time.

She entered the door to Aleysha's apartment. Keeping his face turned her way, Valeron walked on past with the same feigned reluctance at parting. His back crawled with invisible snakes as he went along the hall and down the steps.

NINE

Garden and Boudoir

THE first floor of the palace, like the second, was nearly deserted. Even most guards—never necessary anyhow—had been relieved of duty here, to add to the pomp and splendor of the ceremony in the temple. Valeron saw only three persons: a woman, not a slave, but a servant at whom he winked; a hurrying page who did not even glance at him; a bored soldier.

"Join me in a cup?"

Valeron shook his head, indicated some mission with an important wave of his hand, and went on. With a quick step and a preoccupied air he strode down the side corridor toward the garden. By the time he stepped out into the garden, dripping and fragrant and sparkling from a morning rain, he knew how groundless his apprehension had been.

He did wonder whether that button he had pushed, far below in the vast humming chamber, could have caused rain as well as an extinguishing of lights . . .

The gardens of the Imperial Palace were famed throughout the empire. Lush verdancy surrounded beds of bright flowers and giggling crystal pools with alabaster statues that tumbled sparkling water into their clear depths. Frutescent greenery was cut in ornate designs and arrow-straight rows, shaded only partially by the emerald fronds of well-tended alia trees that bowed with their bounty of saffron fruits. The air was heady with the overwhelming fragrance of a score and more separate perfumes from a rainbow of flowers. Trees, flowers, hedges, and grass glistened with the liquid silver of raindrops.

Beside the rustling verdure of the gardens rose the mighty pile of grayed white stone that was the Imperial

Palace. The structure of the planet's native stones and marble had stood since the time of the Ancients, escaping somehow the awful rampaging wars and cataclysms that had destroyed the machine civilization. From the palace's towering frostiness, triple-arched windows peered disinterestedly down upon the beauty at their feet . . .

—and at the man in cerulean uniform, white cloak, and panache, who had no time to admire the loveliness of the cool greenery and chuckling fountains. A glance about told Valeron car Nadh that he was alone, and he walked down an aisle bordered by head-high shrubbery. The nodding seagreen plumage of uss feathers atop his helm stopped beneath a tall alia tree, turned this way and that.

He saw no one. Valeron sprang up, caught a branch, and swung himself onto it amid a shower of sparkling water from disturbed leaves. With a little smile, he mused that no one had dared climb these sacred-to-the-emperor trees since Aleysha had grown past her tomboy stage!

He clambered up, eyes on one window among the many in the wall a few feet away. The fragrance of fruit, ripe to bursting, teased his nostrils, reminding him of his hunger. His stomach snarled. He plucked two and slipped them within his tunic. With their damp chill against his skin, Valeron laid hold of a branch and began carefully to edge out along the one beneath it.

Once he'd moved as far as he dared on the restless branch, he tensed his legs and slowly crouched. Releasing his grip, he jumped.

He caught himself with talon-curving fingers. His feet clumped onto the ledge that ran around the wall below the windows. For a moment he was sure he had made deadly error; his fingers were sliding on the wet stones, his body commencing to bow backward to fall two stories.

Valeron hung there, slipping. Desperate will and well-toned muscles aided him in lunging forward, spreading his arms. He stood panting against the wall, palms far apart. Again, with great care, he glanced around.

The lack of security appalled him. *Not even the gardener's assistants,* he mused, *work on Coronation Day!* Then he inched along the ledge. Arms widespread, he peered in at the window he remembered as Aleysha's.

A blaze of yellows met his gaze: primrose and jonquil and mustard, old gold and bright aureate and greenish peridot amid beige and coppery orange-yellow. Curtains, hangings, carpet, draperies; all were shades of yellow. Even the crocheted covers on the chocolate-lacquered furniture were the rich color of new bronze. Across the room from the window the somber darkness of a tall paneled door was softened by a lacy arras of pale saffron.

But a few feet away a woman sat with her back to him. The lustrous waterfall of blueblack hair was not Aleysha's, nor was the bare back that was the color of the great cats that roamed the eastward hills of Branarius's main continent. Humming she was while she sewed, facing the door; either she had not heard him or she had decided to pretend.

Valeron's mouth widened in a little smile. That marvelous mass of heavy hair had been combed and brushed since he'd left Jheru at the door a few minutes ago! With another cautious crab-step, he steadied himself in the unpaned arch of the tall window.

Just as Jheru Aleyshanta seemed to become aware of the shadow falling across her back, he flexed his legs and jumped.

His boots struck the carpet behind her chair almost soundlessly and his right hand clamped over her mouth even as he alit. His left arm went under hers at the shoulder and across her back, his hand gripping her other arm just above the elbow.

He raised her from the chair.

"I am a desperate criminal," he growled in her ear. "I am armed, and will not hesitate to double the size of your navel. Scream and be dead."

She did not move. After her first shocked jerk, she remained still. He took his hand from her mouth.

"Barbarian!" she snarled, and behind her he scowled. But she added more: "Well, do rape on me and be done with it, desperate criminal! I know I'm irresistible."

His scowl became a grin. Tightening his fingers on her right arm he turned her—painfully, her arms twisting—to face him. Releasing her arm, his left hand leaped across her back to grasp her other elbow while his right clamped on her left. She had known a brief instant of freedom, but he moved too fast for her to use it. Both arms were squeezed in those huge hands again—squeezed and pulled, for he lifted her body to his and bent his head to lips stained heliotrope with some sweet-smelling cosmetic.

He held her against him, only her toes on the floor, and his mouth bore down on hers. Twisting his head, he fastened teeth into her lower lip just enough to give her a lovepain without breaking the soft skin. There was considerable pressure against his chest; *fine cushions for a man's body she carries about before her*, he thought. After a moment, her lips moved against his in a soft, passion-roused murmur. She tasted like woman, and lust ready ever to flare, and perfume.

He released her with some reluctance. Her heels settled to the floor with a jar. Grinning, he raised a finger to his lips. He nodded at the door behind her.

"Shh—the guard."

"You kiss like a barbarian, barbarian, and you're wet to boot."

"You should not have spoken," he returned challenge, "your breathing is rapid and your voice hoarse."

"I was squeezed half in twain."

"No apology made."

"Hmp!" She showed him a lot of lower lip. "Men should be made to have breasts, so knowledge would be with them of what it is like to have them squashed against a *cuirass!*"

It occurred to Valeron then that he *was* wet, and not where he should be. His stomach—and then he remembered the two golden fruits he'd slipped within his tunic. He put in a hand, felt the sticky mess against his ribs and belly, and withdrew his fingers, with a distasteful face.

"I daren't ask," Jheru said, with arched brows.

The "desperate criminal" fought back laughter. "Fruit. I plucked two alias and slipped them into my tunic. You squashed them."

"*I!*" she said, watching him unfasten the cloak from the hooks on the cuirass, let it drop, start in to open the breast-plate itself. "And what prompted the ferocious kiss the while *I* mashed your fruits—while you mashed mine?"

He dropped the cuirass atop the cloak. "A reward for aiding me."

"*Reward!* Hmp!"

"Punishment, then, for calling me a name with scorn in your voice," he said, busy with his tunic, the front of which was broadly wet-stained.

"One kiss and you begin undressing! My *lord!*"

He looked at her. "You did comb and brush your hair and sit deliberately with your back to the window, girl."

She had no ready answer to that. Carefully he picked up the corners of his tunic and held a wad of cloth at his stomach, knowing she was watching the tightening and loosening and rippling of the massive plates of muscle that were his pectorals—with the same irresist-ible appreciation with which he watched her move.

A shame, he thought, of the time and place. *Sexual animals, both of us.*

"You've been cut," she said. "That's dried blood!"

"Damn. I thought you were admiring the muscle—that's a scratch."

He stepped to the table, where he opened the little bag he'd made of his tunic. It was a messy smear of bright yellow alia skin, clear juices, and snowy pulp. He wiped his chest and hands on the tunic.

"Now," he said, turning to her.

"Now," she said. "It may interest you to know that I could easily have kneed you in the crotch while you played the great barbar role in kissing me. Too, we have no men's clothing here, and probably none in the palace to cover that great bulk—and you hardly look a king waiting to meet his empress."

He took a step and his hand leaped out to clamp onto her wrist.

"Have care, Jheru-the-slave. I *am* king. When were you last beaten?"

She twisted, hurting her own arm, and presented him her back. She raised her hair with her free hand. After giving him a few seconds to gaze at the old whip-stripe there, she turned back.

"I have been," she said, with her teeth together. "I bear that stripe always. He laid the whip high, so my hair would cover the mark and not mar my back—or my *value*." Her eyes met the Branarian's steadily. "I was not so careful with the knife I used on him."

He returned her gaze for a long moment of silence, then nodded, once, and released his grip. If she expected apology or tender word she was mistaken; Valeron had known few and bestowed few. "I believe you," he said. And he added, touching his chest, "And I am bare by choice, *girl*."

Lights of anger played and flashed in the deep black of her eyes while she stared at him. Her mouth tautened. Carefully, staring, she folded her arms over her breasts.

This, he thought, and not without admiration, *is like no slave I have ever encountered!*

As he had done, she nodded briefly, one time. "Aye, my lord King Valeron. My instructions were that I hide you in her room, lest *he* return with her."

She indicated a heavy drape, yellow, with silver threading. It hung in the doorway of an adjoining room. She turned to walk to the drape, and he knew she assumed he would follow. Valeron marveled. He watched her backside appraisingly, thinking that she was surely twitching those broad hips a bit overmuch, until she reached the doorway. He did not follow until she started to turn.

When he had released his grip on her wrist it had gleamed palely, then gone angrily dark as the blood rushed back. It was still red; she had neither glanced at it nor touched it.

"Please remain in here, lord King," she told him

with the same stiffness, "and please be silent." Her eyes as she gazed up at him were chill and hooded, now.

Built luxuriously close to the ground is Jheru, he mused, *with hair dark as night and hips and butt to lull a man to sleep—and a prideful temper!* It likely exploded into sheer savagery when unleashed. *She should have been of Branarius!*

But he did not pay her that compliment aloud, or any other.

His eyes were darting glances about the room as he entered, checking the window, marking possible vantage points in event of trouble. In this sheer reflex, his natural edgeman's appraisal of the terrain, he missed the change in the eyes she held fixed on him, failed to see *her* appraisal.

"My lord King of Branarius does not like my lady's bedchamber?"

"No, nor the mocking tone of her servant. I am minded to buy you and see how you like swinging by your fingers—or pleasuring thirty or forty men, perhaps, save that after being among these mock-men of Carmeis you'd probably enjoy it to swooning. Should I be expected to have comfort with me amid a woman's gauzes and satins and silks and pillows and—fluff? Or a servant's forwardness and lack of respect? Back to your sewing, slave, and sneeze good and loud if I need warning. Oh. I am hungry."

She lowered her head, biting at her lip, but tossed her hair enough to let him know she was not so chastised as she pretended. Jheru left him, and he held back the hand that would have leaped across her well-developed backside. *Likely she expects that*, he thought, watching her pass through the curtains.

Pulling down his brows, he glanced about once more. *Hidden in a woman's bedchamber, by Branar!*

Well . . . it's not the first time.

He disliked the opulence of Aleysha's chamber, the skirted covering of the mirror-mounted table, the gilded scrollwork on the slim-legged chairs—of plast, by the gods!—the flimsy lace of the curtains at the window, the heavy gold of the drapes that framed them. He regarded the bed, which was canopied to make it like unto a bower, a lovenook.

Hmp! For a virgin empress?

The bed was aclutter with pillows of varied shapes and colors; spheres and fat disks and squares and diamond-shapes of indigo and chrysolite and coral and apricot and ultramarine. More satin cushions lay at his feet, and he kicked one flying across the room. Valeron car Nadh of Branarius wondered idly: After the pomp and feminine beauty of her present surroundings, could the soft Princess Aleysha be satisfied as co-ruler of a newly born outworld state? Or happy in the bedchamber *he* would have, were he abiding in this palace?

But he shook his head at the latter thought, for no desire for the imperial crown was with him.

He dropped to the bed, noting without pleasure its luxuriant bounce. Stretching out, he nestled his broad back amid caressing pillows. His spurs sliced the pink silk of the spread; the sweat from his body stained it.

He half-rose when the curtains parted; into the room flew cloak and cuirass and wadded tunic. "I'm off to seek a fresh tunic," Jheru said. "No one will come."

"And food!"

He lay back with a grin. The dusky hue of that girl—*girl nothing, that's a woman, and on Branarius she'd be a mother several times over*—reminded him of the golden-eyed rock-cats of his world; *I'd make wager on other similarities, as well!*

What to do? Somehow commandeer a ship and get back to Branarius ... raise a force of his already battle-weary men ... come hurtling back to attack Darcus Cannu with fire and sword and ax ...

In thought, he stared at the lamps hanging above his head.

From the ceiling they shed the deathless soft light of the Ancients' magic. Never dimmed, even by the ages, seven lamps swung from twisted chains of delicate gold filigree. Each was an unseamed teardrop of opaque crystal that bore the topographic markings of one of the seven worlds. Valeron recognized Branarius and he stared at it, thinking.

The long tense wait in the dungeon and his trekking of the pit, the sword-wielding meetings with metal serpent and Shanaru ... these joined with the mesmeric quality of the soft light to lull him to sleep.

TEN

Empress and Warlord

THE sound of a single step was enough to rouse a man raised by the Sungoli.

Valeron was off the bed and across the room with sword in hand seconds after he heard someone enter the adjoining chamber. He heard voices: Aleysha's—and Darcus Cannu's, as she took her leave of him at the corridor door. For a moment Valeron entertained the very pleasant thought of bursting through the drapes and pushing Aleysha aside to shove his sword's thirsty length into the traitorous prime minister's guts.

He shook his head. That would accomplish Cannu's death, aye, but his own as well. A glance at the chair beside him discovered the fresh uniform-tunic there. Hurriedly he set by the sword and shrugged into the pale blue garment. Just as he finished, he heard a whispered consultation in the other room. Then Aleysha was sweeping aside the hangings that separated the rooms.

Velquen's daughter was magnificent; the word "striking" was inadequate. Her imperially seagreen tresses were piled high in an intricate network of coils, laced with lustrous pearls and sparkling gold thread. Around that pearl-and-gold and foam pile of hair rested the golden circlet, with its six rising points, each surmounted by a small sphere of pure silver. Jewels flashed from a heavy carcanet that spread fanlike from her throat onto her chest, above twin pressure points of small conical breasts. They thrust against a gown of pearl-sewn white satin, heavily brocaded.

Over her shoulders and down her back to her heels swept the bluegreen mantle of the sea's foam; imperium on seven planets.

It struck him at that moment, gazing at this glittering beauty, this regal daughter of an emperor, of civilization:

I am Valeron the Mighty, barbarian edgeman. My black throne I won with my own dripping sword and my muscle. I am a ruler, called Warlord because those I rule are ever warlike. We won our place over the Sungoli by wading through a sea of blood, a tangled Sargasso of corpses. Warlord! *A barbarous title for the barbarous ruler of a barbarous world!*

He stared at her. A wide belt of gem-set silver lamé circled her waist, a sparkling point rising to her abdomen, another pointing down a flat stomach that widened into delicately molded hips.

My lord Barbarian, Darcus Cannu called me.

Her face was serene. Around her neck hung the imperial necklace, more important by tradition than scepter or crown: a delicate golden chain supported a huge white pearl. It lay in the broad valley between her breasts, below the carcanet, nestled against fitted brocade of milkwhite satin. From that pearl radiated six lengths of still golden chain, each connected to a smaller pearl. And each of those was linked similarly together; Carmeis in the center, around it the Six Worlds, inseparably linked one to the other, and all to the imperial planet, the hub.

"My . . . lady."

So she was. This beautiful vision of bejeweled, satin, brocaded loveliness, this delicate body with its slender, almost angular hips and dainty cones of bosom, raised amid silk and velvet and precious stones and metals, delicate foods and liveried, obedient servants in this awesome palace . . . this was not little Leysha.

She was Aleysha, first empress of the Seven Worlds of Carmeis.

At his words, finely arched brows rose to curve still higher above dark eyes widened by deep green liner. "Last time you called me 'Little Leysha' and pulled my hair," she reminded him, and lips etched with lilac lifted slightly at the corners.

I am dirty. Dirty, abraded, in need of a shave—again. I am here direct from a dungeon cell and two en-

counters to the death. On my hands must be the reek of Shanaru's blood. He fought to keep from raising those big hands to his nostrils.

Suddenly he felt the gulf between himself and this woman, and he was shy, speechless. For perhaps the first time in his life Valeron admitted the importance of the difference between himself and his people and— others, those born to civilized ways. On this world and in this presence, Valeron car Nadh the Mighty felt less than adequate.

"Last time—six years ago—you were not ... Empress."

"Nor was I a woman. But—last night in the darkness you treated me as a woman, and . . ."

She broke off in uncertain hesitation, and he realized that this new commander of Empire held her eyes on his only with difficulty. *She is far less certain of herself than I,* he thought. And: *She is as shy as I, and as short of words!* When she went on, he knew it was with difficulty:

"And promised," Aleysha said, "to do better when there were no bars between us."

She is pale, he thought, *pale and lovely as the marble faces of the caryatids in the throne-room.* "I—"

"More speech? Surely, my lord Valeron, surely you are a man of your word."

He spoke no more; he gave her no more words. The snowy brocade crumpled against his chest. Her lips were cool and very soft and very yielding as he pulled her against him, gathering her in, surrounding her with his arms, while he surrounded her mouth with his. His mouth enveloped the sweet softness of hers. Her palms —smooth and soft as a woman's thighs—moved up to lie against the hard roundness of his shoulders. He tasted salt and realized it was a tear. Breathing more heavily, he eased the pressure of his arms about her.

"Oh Valeron," she stammered, childlike, and he held her to him and breathed the fragrance of her hair.

Does anyone really change? the barbarian wondered. *Do little girls ever really grow up? Do fiery youths ever really change while hair commences to gray and smooth youthful muscles become corded bands and lines form*

*on our faces like erosion channels on a hillside? Have
we really changed, Aleysha and I? Is she so different?
Or—is she the same, in different clothes, with jewels—
playing the part of empress . . . playing the role of
woman?*

While she clung to him his eyes caught movement
behind her; Jheru was peeping at them through the
draperies. Valeron stared. Jheru vanished.

The girl who had become an empress pushed back
from him, raised slim fingers to lift the crown from her
head. She dropped it onto his cloak, forgotten in a pile
of fabric on the floor. With her hands still raised to her
pile of hair, she turned her back to him. She arched her
neck forward so that he looked down upon wispy hair
the color of the sea's pale, pale foam against a smooth
olive neck, a neck without the mark of the whip's kiss.

"This awful heavy collar, Valeron. Unclasp it,
please."

He did so, drawing the carcanet from her and marveling at its weight, automatically speculating on its
worth. Her hands left her hair. As she turned back to
him, he could not help his gasp.

Pearls fell rattling to the floor and a frothy cloud of
hair like silk fell to wreathe her face. It caressed her
brocaded shoulders, streamed down upon one firm
small breast. It was not the robe of marmoreal white
that sheathed her in shining glory, he saw. It was that
marvelous cloud of hair, so pale-dyed. He raised his
hands to touch its strands: threads of silk between his
fingers.

Aleysha hurled the heavy belt from her and heaved a
great breath. She smiled through the tears that glistened
in her eyes and stained her cheeks: the sun bursting
through the clouds. Her arms rose to his shoulders. Her
deep inhalation filled her lungs and strutted her chest to
push her against him so that he felt the warmth of her
through the layers of cloth.

"Kiss me again," she said in a tiny voice from the
throat.

He did without question, enveloping her mouth with
his while she pressed hard against him.

Drawing her head back, she leaned against his encircling arms to look up at him through lowered lashes that were a tenuous shield. "The kisses of the man I loved when I was a child . . . the kisses of the conqueror of Branarius . . . and the conqueror of Aleysha," she said. She lowered her head to lean against him, her face against his chest. "I have cast off the symbols of Empire," she said softly, "all save this awful stiff gown of cold satin . . ."

He held her, hearing her words, realizing that this was invitation; an oblique, shy invitation from a girl who'd not yet had time to become accustomed to being a woman. *No experience is with her to make herself as sure as an empress should be—or to act as sure, whether she is or no.*

Thoughts charged rampant through his mind; thoughts of this slim young woman and the softness of her, and the unusual firmness of the apples of her chest, warm against him. He thought of the great throne downstairs in that magnificent long hall. A downward glance showed him the crown of Empire at his feet. He thought irresistibly of the soft bed behind him.

Valeron remembered no other occasion when he had debated so, when he had been so assailed by so many provoking thoughts, so many considerations beyond his own.

What ails me? Has this damned beast with many arms we call 'civilization'—with awe upon us—got hold of me?

Her father is dead, he told himself. *Murdered. And the man who should have become instantly her protector is the murderer, a traitor. Now some of the strain, the tenseness is leaving her—and flowing into me! Flowing into the arms and body of the big barbar hero she remembers romantically from sunnier days. No,* he thought. *It is no question of right or wrong; she offers me what Branarian girls eagerly and anxiously yield up at twelve and earlier. It is question of myself, and herself, and what we might be.*

And he decided: he would allow—even force—her to maintain her defenses.

She is not of Branarius. I shall not answer invitation with action that may do more infatuation on her—and

later drive a wedge between us. When the bright sun of
warmth and happiness again shines on Carmeis and the
throne, Empire and Aleysha ...

"I am returning to Branarius," he murmured into a
tiny ear, as if he had not heard her. "I shall raise an
army to drive Darcus Cannu into the ground and tell
the truth to the Council of Kings; to set that crown
firmly on your head."

Again she leaned back in his arms, looked into his
eyes with disappointment in her own. "Take me with
you! Take me from here!"

"I cannot. If I take you with me there will be no one
on the throne—and Darcus Cannu will dispatch ships
to the kings at once, saying that I have done kidnap on
you. They will descend on Branarius like a swarm of
beetles after an over-mild winter, and my own people
will suffer. No, Aleysha. I cannot take you with me.
You must remain here. On Branarius I have loyal men,
and from there I can visit the other worlds and tell
them what has happened. They will come—all of us together. Darcus Cannu cannot stand against us all."

"You—intend to bring—*the kings* here ... to overcome Darcus?" The gown rippled with the tempo of her
breathing.

"Overcome? We'll stretch his skinny neck a dozen
centimeters! How do you think the kings will take my
news?"

"I—I hadn't thought of bringing them into it ..."
She gazed at his chest, frowning.

"They *are* in it," he said, even while his eyes inspected hips so gently rounded and wondered about the
shape of legs and backside beneath the stiff fabric.
"Their emperor has been murdered. Aleysha: years ago
I made vow to your father to march against any who
sought to dethrone him or cause dissent among the
worlds. I came here to renew that oath, the oath each
of the other kings has taken ... to protect all against
one's becoming an aggressor. I keep my vows, and so
will they—even though it means attacking Carmeis
City."

He sat down on the edge of the bed, pulling her
down with him. "You are Empress of the Seven Worlds

of Carmeis. But the empire is scattered through space, and not so closely knit, nor is any king so powerful that he need not fear the others. Sid-Alors ... Maruthia ... Ghulan ... Lavian ... Nyor ... and now Branarius. Each ruled by its own native sovereign. What if Maruthia and Lavian attacked Carmeis? The capital, the hub of the wheel that is Empire—it would be in need of help! That is the reason for the oath. That's why the kingdoms are palatinates, why the kings bend creaky knees to the occupant of the throne here. And the person of the empress herself is at this moment ... under a state of siege!"

He came to pause; she but listened, saying nothing, nodding.

"I must return for my armies, Aleysha, and I admit no desire is with me to leave you."

"But ... if you lead your men against Carmeis ... will *you* not be besieging us?"

"I have thought of that. But no. I'd be coming to *free* Carmeis, and I'd make that clear and obvious by bending a knee to you when all is over. Perhaps it may not be necessary, Aleysha. Darcus Cannu must be sensible enough to back down when he knows he faces the combined power of the Five—the *Six* Kings, including me. But if he does not—it is our duty to your father and to you to conquer him. To smash him."

His hand fisted. She gazed at that club of flesh and bone. And she nodded.

"Aye," Aleysha said with a deep, heaving sigh. "I must stay. Loyalty to me, to my father is still with many, and—" She lifted her chin, firming it. "I am emperor—empress. It is my ... duty to remain here. I can postpone marriage with Darcus. So long as I do, I am safe."

Valeron bit his lip, again at the pondering. He stared over her shoulder, out the window. At last he released his grip on her arms. He looked down at her.

"It will not be long, Aleysha. Yet ... each of the worlds is two days apart, and two days' journey from Carmeis—that's fourteen days in travel alone. With more time necessary to explain, to get them together, to organize, to load ships . . . it may perhaps be as long as twenty-and-five days, Aleysha."

"Too long," she said, nestling her face against his chest once more. "But—I shall think of something. I'll wait, Valeron. I—I'll be waiting."

When he lifted her chin to kiss her again, he felt her shiver against him.

Then she became an empress. She talked rapidly.

"I shall write a letter to Lexton of Maruthia—not dictate; I shall write it myself. And Jheru will go with you, to show you where your men are kept. You must not send her back—he would certainly find a way to wrest truth from her. And she will be of value to you, with Lexton. I'll swear she was kidnaped."

He smiled. "The kidnaping of that one might well require myself and two others!"

But she had risen, all business, to go and bend over her dressing-table. She entered lines of characters on a piece of thin rush-paper with her quill; lines of characters unintelligible to the Warlord of Branarius. The pen scratched in a final flourish. She breathed on the paper, and struck flint and steel to light a candle. After dripping the tallow on the folded sheet of paper, she rolled her ring across it. She turned to hand him the paper, regarding the ring.

"My first imperial letter," the empress said, with wonder in her voice, and awe. "And I wrote it myself!"

From an ornately carved box on the dressing-table she took a ring. "This was my tenth birthday present, from Lexton. Show it him."

Valeron accepted and regarded it, a flowery circlet of silver with excellent workmanship. It would not pass the joint on his smallest finger.

Aleysha was walking across the room, straight and tall and willowy, her hair billowing about her shoulders like windswept waves. She spoke but a few words to the young woman in the other room. She returned slowly, her eyes on his as he sat on the edge of her pillow-strewn bed in the tunic of a Palatine Guardsman.

"Suddenly cold is with me, Valeron. Cold, and fright. Did you know that this morning all the lights—the *Ancient lights*—went out? For less than a minute, and then they were there again." She glanced up at the seven globes above her head. "But much fear was with us, all of us. Wherever you were, finding your way here ... you knew no fear, did you?"

Aye, the Warlord of Branarius thought, *fear was with me too—but for a different reason!* And he renewed decision to keep his counsel about what he'd found below.

"Fear is with me, Valeron, and I must not admit it to anyone until you return. Fear, and cold." She stood before him. "Warm me, Valeron! Oh warm me before you leave me, that I may cherish your warmth and strength until you return!"

And Valeron's resolves came crashing down like siege-mined walls. He warmed Aleysha, and empress became woman thereby.

ELEVEN

Sword and Spaceship

A TIPSY warrior and his close-snuggled blowze tottered toward the windowless block of stone that housed the Branarian prisoners. The square prison was outside the city, just over a kilometer from the shipfield. Daily the barbarian captives had been taunted by their guards—and by the hissing whooshes of the big ships coming and going. Five guards remained on duty, day and night. None expected a direct frontal attack; their number indicated their commander's respect for the outworlders.

No suspicion was done on the sentries by the weaving approach of a drunken Palatine and his woman of the evening. The soldiers snickered at the big fellow's condition; the girl they goggled. She was obviously a slave; her bosom was bare; and there was a pleasant plentitude of it to bare. Her navel winked darkly above the emerald kirtle slung low on wide dark hips.

When the couple was but a couple of meters away, one of the guards opened his mouth to say something—and the man whipped back his cloak to drive at them with a naked sword of appalling length.

Both sentries at the prison's front leveled their halberds with a speed commendable for men whose eyes had been on a more-than-pretty young woman. Yet the attacker's charge was already in progress. Striking aside the foremost pike with his sword, Valeron stepped between them to seize the second. He yanked. Its wielder staggered forward, and Valeron lopped off his right hand at the wrist. Blood spurted as the fellow dropped his weapon to grasp the spurting stump. His eyes rolling up, he fainted in pain and shock. His blood pumped out on the ground in a scarlet river.

The other stiffened and collapsed—with Jheru's dagger in his throat.

While he snatched up the keys and fitted them into the lock, Valeron gave her a look. What a woman this was! He'd seen Branarian women with less nerve. She was calmly wiping her serpent-bladed kris on the dead man's tunic, her hips flaring out into big pillows as she squatted. Built like a warrior was Aleysha, and but a kitten in bed; built for bed was Jheru—and a warrior!

"I retract the threat to swing you by your fingers, Jehru, if you retract the mockery in your voice when you said the word 'barbarian.'"

Jehru glanced up to give him a completely serious look from those black eyes. "I—meant no mockery, my lord. I do not disrespect you."

Valeron was surprised at the quietly spoken words, particularly in view of her former attitude. He bobbed his head in a single swift nod. "Good. You are one with us of Branarius. And—"

There was no time for him to finish; no time for her to answer. The brief rencontre with the guards had not been silent, and the other three sentries now came boiling around the building. Valeron whirled, sword up and out from his body, ready for a vicious swipe or the lunge he executed all to well.

The key slid from the lock and dropped to the ground.

Valeron car Nadh stood his ground, legs apart, one heel at the brink of a spreading pool of crimson. The charging Carmeians saw his readiness and slowed, wide-eyed glances leaping from him to their sprawled comrades to the waiting edgeman once more. Then, stepping forward cautiously and in semi-crouches, they moved on him. The trio moved apart at the same time, to come at him from three sides.

Behind the Branarian, key clicked in lock.

Jheru let go the key to skip aside as the outworlders swarmed forth, blinking. The first man free snatched up a sword from one of the fallen Carmeians and was at Valeron's side in one long stride.

The three Carmeian soldiers halted, staring; this man was bald, and possessed glaring, flaming, golden eyes

whose stare was unabated by lashes and brows. He was
an animalistic apparition for the frightening of children—and Carmeian sentries.

"Yah Branarii!"

The three Carmeians went down in terribly short order.

A few minutes later a female slave of about eighteen
years, a man in the uniform of the imperial bodyguard,
and twenty stubbly-faced outworlders swarmed over the
military post at the shipfield. And one golden-eyed,
hairless, ferocious—man?

Valeron's lieutenant swung to grasp rein and saddle
of a nervous horse. "That ship at the launch rack, my
lord—I'll hold it!"

And he and three others mounted the horses of the
downed gate-guards to gallop across the shipfield.

The outworlders spurred their mounts precariously
up the loading ramp of the big ship that lay there, its
sleek nose space-aimed. The three Carmeians at the top
of the incline stared at the oncoming horses, gauged the
distance between themselves and the ship's port. Then
they swarmed down the girders to the ground.

With cries of "Yah Branarii!" the mounted Branarians stormed into the ship.

Very impolitely ushering out the just-boarded passengers, the outworlders took over the spacer. Burgon car
Burgon went back out onto the platform and looked
down. His lips clamped; such violence and carnage he
saw was surely unprecedented, here on the imperial
shipfield!

The ground below was strewn with Carmeian soldiers
of the shipfield detachment, dead or writhing in pools of
their own curdling blood. The ship's former passengers
streamed across the field toward the gate in full yelling
flight, along with a crowd of stevedores; the attacking
Branarians had un-barbarically exercised care to touch
not one civilian. Two-score men from the Barbarian
World—and a girl-woman mainly naked—came charging up the ramp, their rear covered by four of their
number. Those backed slowly upward, hacking viciously at the pursuit.

Prefect Burgon bowed as Valeron came onto the platform.

"Your private ship is ready, my lord," he said with a grin. "The former passengers have graciously agreed to await another, and our men are even now changing course for Branarius."

Valeron stood aside while his men and Jheru streamed aboard. "Most kind of you, Burgon. Do you remind me to send official apology to the former passengers. And our thanks."

The Branarian rear-guard glanced up, saw that the others were aboard, and turned to spring up the ramp. The last man turned, aimed briefly, and launched his blooded Carmeian sword at the pursuers as if it were a spear. He watched with satisfaction as it sent one Carmeian, desperately dodging, toppling off the ramp. Then he turned flashing golden eyes to Valeron with an animal smile that bared a double row of animal teeth.

"Sanxarkhl will understand when I say it is pleasure to be allowed again to slay the Hairmen I was taught to hate?"

Valeron dropped a hand on the Sungol's shoulder. "I understand. So long as you can tell the difference between them and us, Rankhnax," he said, and Rankhnax's grin broadened.

They swung into the ship, Valeron and Burgon securing first one port, then the other.

Setting course for Branarius involved pulling one lever and depressing a few buttons. The pursuing Carmeians felt the tremor of the catwalk as the spacer awoke with the pushing of the final key. With looks of horror, they spun about and went rushing and sliding back down the ramp. They had not quite reached bottom when the catwalk was hurled into the air and heated backwash swept over them with terrible force.

The shuttle-ship shuddered, started to slide upward, then seemed to spring into the air. It vanished then, as centuries-old solar engines proved once again the infallibility of the Ancients and the god Siense.

While tramping boots rushed to inform him of the escape of the Branarians, the Imperial Prime Minister kneeled on the carpet of his office. He touched the brownish stain with a diffident finger, held it up to examine its tip. He squinted. Placing both palms flat on the floor, he bent his head low to sniff. And he looked around with a frown.

"Blood," he muttered, "mopped up . . . "

Darcus Cannu's anthracitic eyes searched for more. There! Another spot: the tiny stain of a mere droplet. And here another—against the paneled wall.

Strange . . . the spot was not a full one; a half-drop snugged against the wall. Yet none marked the wood panel! Darcus Cannu frowned anew. Slowly he got to his feet, still frowning, his thin lips pursed. He gazed thoughtfully at the wall.

When he had ordered the purple drapes hung there, both for decoration and to enhance the room's warmth, he had ordered the handsome paneled section left bare. He had liked it—and thought that someday he'd hang a sword and shield or escutcheon there. When one had at last been granted, he'd liked it better on the other wall. He had never examined this wall, never thought about the handsome inset of wood, which he'd thought of as purely decorative. One did not bother examining the walls of one's office. Nor did anyone know aught of secret doors in the palace.

Could it be . . . He rapped on the paneling with bony knuckles. Then again, harder. His expression changed at the sound; there was no stone behind this panel!

The prime minister examined it, going over it with eyes and fingers, and soon he was drawing back the violet draperies to peer and feel at the bare stone. And now that he had something to look for, he found it.

When sheepish, excited Palatines arrived to report, Darcus Cannu had departed his office—though not via its normal door.

TWELVE

Slave and Elder

LEXTON of Maruthia was the acknowledged leader of the Five Kings; it was toward Maruthia that the newly-commissioned flagship of Branarius—the *Empress Aleysha*—turned her sleek nose less than two days after her master had reached the barbarian planet.

Behind them the field was covered by a thousand archers; another two thousand edgemen awaited. If Darcus Cannu dared attempt invasion, his men would be dead on their own ramps.

Aboard the *Empress Aleysha* were Valeron, High Counselor Saldon, Jheru of Carmeis, and a cortège of thirty scarlet-cloaked warriors of Branarius.

To protect his own peace of mind, Valeron had magnanimously given the slave permission to wear an upper garment. Her choice was worse than the mandatory slave-nudity on Carmeis; she wore a black halter whose four ends were tied in a knot at the top of her rib cage and another behind her neck. The garment's color merely made fairer and enhanced the roundness of those outsize hemispheres of tawny flesh that crowded each other for space in the halter's V. Valeron vowed that she bounced them deliberately; and *she*, he had growled to Saldon, called *him* unfeeling barbarian!

Quite naturally, grinning, Rankhnax had asked his "brother," Sanxarkhl–Valeron, how she was. The Sungoli warrior had frowned and continued frowning, staring, when Valeron told him he had not couched her. Rankhnax indicated a certain fear concerning the effect of "civilization" on the big Hairman whom he considered a Sungol.

Jheru had not been aboard one of the long cadmium-colored spacers since she was a child, and she said so. She was brushing her hair, a mass like a torrent of ink splashing past her shoulders.

"What makes them go?"

"We know not," Valeron told her. Seated in the spaceship's control chamber he was lavishing a link-by-link inspection on his mailcoat and did not look up; he well knew the effect the brushing motion of her arms had upon the halter. "They have always gone. None has ever failed. We merely push buttons and the ships do all else."

She tossed her hair. "And if we know not what makes them *go*, how is knowledge with us to set course?"

Valeron shrugged and nodded at Saldon. The Elder's white head was bent over the instrument console, and he turned it to raise a white eyebrow at the girl.

"Nor do we know what makes the Ancient lights glow. They do, and we use them. We know much of our ancestors, girl, and we know little. Knowledge is with us that our empire was called a 'solar system' and that it was artificially created. The Ancients somehow dragged great chunks of rock through space . . . set them here." Making a vague gesture, Saldon looked embarrassed at his own lack of knowledge.

"The Six Worlds are identical in size and mass and 'gravity'—that is what the Ancients called air, we believe. It means a man weighs the same on every world. Each 'satellite' is twelve thousand three hundred kilometers across. A kilometer is about twenty-five hundred of our paces. The—"

"Their measure was a—a *kilometer*, and it was—whatever you said? An odd number of paces?" She chuckled. "The ancients were strange people indeed! Why not exactly two thousand, or three, or *any* even number?"

Saldon shrugged. "They were a complicated people."

"Their paces were different from ours," Valeron said, eyes on armor. It clinked as he moved the link chain slowly through his fingers. "One broken link can be death," he'd been taught, and his experience had made him believe.

"At any rate," Saldon said, "the Ancients somehow

'whittled' the worlds to size, somehow set them to travel through space around Carmeis—as Carmeis spins about the sun."

"Carmeis *moves*? Branarius *moves*?" Jheru looked as if she wanted to laugh in his face.

"She knows nothing, son of Nadh. How can I do explanation on an idiot who interrupts with her knowless babble?"

Valeron shrugged and smiled. "You explained it to me, Saldon. I believe you, as I believe that this ship goes. But I cannot explain either."

"You are an Elder who has dedicated his life—and what a lifetime—to Siense, and study of His ways, and the Ancients," Jheru said with more asperity than petulance. "It does no kindness on you to call me names because I have not studied. Why should men not weigh the same everywhere? Very well; Carmeis moves then. But the ships . . ."

Saldon was staring at her. "You have a sharp tongue, slavegirl of Carmeis," he told her. "What you want is the flat of a blade—or its point." He pointed at the sword that Valeron held out to inspect before returning to its care; he was carefully picking out the blood-alley. "But . . . because I am an Elder and have lived these many years—as you so impolitely point out—I can afford to be . . . charitable. I will do fun on you no more."

Valeron shot him a look of surprise. Why—that was almost an apology! *He'd* never got so much from Saldon! So the Elder was susceptible, too . . . Perhaps he was not so old and totally Siense-minded after all; perhaps the joggling of that black bosom-sling did effect on him, too. Valeron glanced at Jheru. Showing no surprise, she accepted the words of the Elder High Counsellor of Branarius as if she were due mollification, even apology!

Valeron's chest heaved in a sigh and he returned to the meticulous checking of each several link of his mail. Into his mind all unbidden stole a thought that did no credit to his empress—or to him for the thinking of it.

This big-built girl-woman who twitted me and did death on a sentry with no qualm that showed and now

*speaks up to Saldon and gains lighter words . . . what a
difference between her and her empress! Jheru'd be no
passive, accepting vessel in the couching, I wager, as
her mistress was . . .*

The Warlord of Branarius gave his mail much attention then, in seeking to banish such doubly unworthy
thoughts from his mind.

"The ships are but shuttle craft," Saldon was saying.
"They cannot quit this system of worlds to—sail among
the stars. Our sun is a star and there are others, you
know. Thousands. Man used to travel among them."

"The *stars? Really?*"

Saldon closed his eyes and smiled. "Aye, 'reeeelly!' "
he said. "Where do you think Mother is?"

"I—I always thought of Mother as . . . myth," Jheru
said, nervous lest she offend a servant of Siense with
heresy.

"And Siense? Do you think He a myth, too, O wise
slavegirl?"

"Oh *no!*" She made the sign in the air; a pair of
crossed ellipses. "*He* exists!"

"Then you are wrong," the old man told her, "on
both counts."

Valeron chuckled.

"Mother is our planet of origin," Saldon went on.
"Long and long ago. Our ancestors were colonists from
a world on which not quite *all* the people were dark of
skin and hair. And . . . Siense is no god."

Young woman into girl on the instant, Jheru made
the ward-sign.

"Oh stop," Saldon bade her. "Siense is . . . a word. A
word of knowledge . . . and Knowledge is no god,
either."

"Valeron! Do you believe him?" she squeaked. "This
heretic priest?"

"Hush," Valeron told her. "I believe what I can see,
feel, hear, taste, Jheru. I speak to Siense . . . when I
am in sore trouble. Otherwise . . . " He shrugged. "You
asked for information, knowledge. Listen to Saldon,
woman. He has it."

"Elder Saldon, I am a slave and have ever been a

slave. I know little. I would have information from your vast store."

The two men gazed at her in considerable surprise, if not shock. In a wholly different tone and manner, Saldon spoke—directly to her, now.

"Valeron's tactics that did defeat on the Sungoli are Siense, gir—Jheru. What runs this ship is Siense also, and so perhaps too is that which makes a silly young female half-cover her body and continue to put brush to hair long after it is lustrous as a silken cloak; perhaps that too is a sort of Siense." His lined face creased scores of time with his smile.

Jheru paused in her brushing. She glared.

"Our ships have but seven possible courses," Saldon told her. He tapped the console. "Here are seven buttons; one for each world. One sets a dial—this one—to prepare. No, don't put question on me as to what that means—I am not sure. One sets this lever for the same purpose, and one feels the vibrations begin. One pushes this button or that; note you that the third is depressed and alit now; that button signifies Maruthia. Nor can we change course. This red button sounds the alarm horn, to secure all doors. One then depresses both these squared buttons simultaneously—to send the ship aloft. Somehow it then uses the sun to fly itself to its destination. There it lands itself and . . . turns itself off. One then pulls this bar back, and all levers and buttons are dead. That is all there is to it. It is not magic, and it is not something sent by the gods. It is the product of wisdom of the Ancients, long lost to us since the Wrath."

Jheru was nodding slowly, licking her lips, staring with flitting eyes at the console. "Could . . . could we not set course for . . . somewhat else?" She waved a plump tawny arm, vaguely. "Not one of the Seven Worlds, I mean. The, uh . . . the sky?"

Saldon smiled. "Space. It is called outer space. This we traverse among the worlds of Empire is inner space, we believe. Aye, we could if we knew how. But these ships are *set*, moulded like a bit of jewelry that can assume no other form—like an emery wheel that can turn in but one direction and cannot move sideward."

Jheru smiled at the mental picture he created with

that analogy. And she kept her gaze fastened on him, and listened attentively in a way that impressed Saldon greatly. A—a *girl*, not even yet a woman, and a slave at that... what an attentive student! He'd had few such. Studying her, he reflected with some nervousness.

Her mind is quick, and she fights, Valeron says—and I believe she has much care for him. And those things he said of the complacency and passiveness of the empress ... it were better for Valeron, and Aleysha—and Jheru—were she not on this ship with us, ever in contact with Valeron. She has the look of a breeding machine about her—just the sort of woman he has ever favored!

"Elder?"

"Uh— the ships have seven destinations," he said in response to her prompting, "and seven only. We dare not do tampering on them until we know more. They might slice off into the sun, or—explode."

"Explode?"

"Fly apart with much noise, like a volcano, worse than a hundred windstorms at once."

Jheru shuddered. "It is that which befell the Ancients!"

"Aye. They controlled the ships and the lights and much else—the weather we think. They controlled Siense— Stop! If you make the sign again I shall petition my lord to decree that you clothe yourself as a slave of Carmeis—*un*clothe yourself!" he corrected. He watched her shoot a glance at Valeron, who had become much more occupied with his mail than before. Saldon said, "Their weapons were terrible beyond belief and understanding. A man could be killed at a great distance, a castle exploded, a mountain moved. Aye. And one day ... war came. There was horror and much death, and people began to slay their Elders, their men of Siense, blaming them for their own evil. They slew and slew and slew in an insane orgy of vengeance upon those who had brought them knowledge." Saldon shook his snowy head.

"Men have ever been fools," the Elder went on quietly. "And so they knew no longer how to operate their own machines. How to heat their houses or cool them through the old magic, and they slipped backward. We believe they even had means of talking among the worlds. All such knowledge died; men slipped backward. Slowly at first, and then faster and faster, as a ship seems to hesitate before it leaps off-world. And—they forgot. Men became little more than savage animals, girl, forced to return to sword and arrow for their constant doing of death on one another."

Valeron lifted his head. "Find me," he said, "*find me one Ancient-weapon, Saldon, and I shall end the doing of death!*"

Saldon smiled at him as a mother smiles upon her impetuous child. "Oh aye, aye, you will end it all. I can do assurance on you that every war fought has been the last; every weapon man invented was the Ultimate Weapon, the one to end all wars forever!" He shook his head. "It is not so. One thing leads to the next. One terrible weapon gives way to another; one man or tribe or nation is supreme until another finds a better means of doing destruction. Those machines I believe the Ancients must have used to melt and fuse earth and rock: think of *their* horror, lord King, as *weapons*. Possession was with them of a hand weapon that was little more than a firemaker, a tool with which to cut steel as though it was fresh butter. But it had other uses. Naught but a little black cylinder with a tiny appendage to squeeze. Soon the Ancients learned they would fry men very nicely."

Something tickled at Valeron's mind. He stared at Saldon, remembering. A pile of bones, turning to dust at his touch . . . Kabir, Jagadis R. . . . Valeron's eyes widened. A small black cylinder— Gods! In his fear and stupidity he had seen such . . . had left it lying on the floor of that chamber beneath the Imperial Palace on Carmeis! A weapon of fire! He stared at the bulkhead opposite, mentally cursing himself.

And a new apprehension that was like unto fear came upon the Warlord of Branarius. *Branar and Lady Aria keep Darcus Cannu from finding that cylinder of the Ancients! Keep him from the room-that-moves and the passage beneath!*

"—here we are," Saldon was saying to Jheru, with-

out noticing Valeron's reaction. "Sword-armed men ...
barbarians indeed! But *all* of us, not just we of Branarius, so long called the Barbarian World. Sword-armed
men, Jheru, concerned with their mail-coats, counseled
by so-called wise men called Elders—for we are really
stupid men indeed—living under ages-old lights and
riding from world to world in ships built in the mists of
pasts. Ships whose mechanisms we understand not at
all! We have not even a proper choice of destination!"

There was silence in the control chamber of the hurtling spacer. All three of them mulled the confusion of
thoughts that twisted like restless serpents in their
minds.

Then Jheru shook her head, vehemently, as if physi-
cally to clear it of thoughts incomprehensible. She said,
"But ... surely Darcus Cannu's men have already
landed on Maruthia."

Saldon blinked. "You absorb all I have said and return to the immediate as if you had not heard
miracles!"

"They concern us, Elder. Perhaps we will regain the
old knowledge, or some of it—slowly at first and then
more rapidly, as you say it was lost. But . . . for the
Now, there are other matters." She spoke the name of
the greatest traitor the empire had ever known as
though it were an obscenity. "*Darcus Cannu.*"

Saldon sighed and returned to the console. She was
right. Here was a startlingly good mind, he mused.
But—so soon over, this discussion, without discussion
at all. How he longed to talk with the Siense-oriented
King of Nyor, young Jallad car Ahmir!

"Surely they have," Valeron said, picking with a tiny
wood-handled tool at Jimarah's complicated hilt. He
did not look up.

Jheru had ceased her brushing. She looked at the big
man as if she suspected he had just fled the Imperial
Lunatorium. "What? Surely what has what?"

"You said that surely Darcus Cannu had landed men
on Maruthia ere now. And I say that surely that is
true."

"But—is that all you have to say?"

Saldon whipped his head around, scraggly white brows pulled down. "Careful with your talk, blowze!"

Her eyes flashed at him. "What's a blowze?"

"A ruddy-faced *wench!*"

"Surely not true of you," Valeron said smiling, "so please refrain from clawing my High Counsellor." He turned the smile on the latter. "Let her talk, Saldon. She is a very valuable blowze, and no woman has talked up to me for years—they but spread their thighs. She is very clever too, not to mention nice to look upon. And—handy with a dagger."

"Too nice to look upon," the Elder said. "On a ship full of men, girl, you were cleverer to cover yourself to the chin."

"Just what sort of reception do you expect on Maruthia, my lord?" she asked, obviously having decided to pretend that Saldon did not exist, with his heresy and his sharp tongue and store of unfamiliar words.

Valeron shrugged. "Chilly, if not worse. I expect we will be met with drawn swords. Fortunately Lexton is not like us; no *barbarian,* he. His men will not kill us out of hand and rape you. Lexton will control that—and then he have to give listen to us." He watched the dark look of worry on her face. "The letter from the empress, with her seal and that ring—those will gain us a hearing. Then it is up to us. Saldon talks better than I. No harm will be done on us."

She shook her head. "Gladness is with me that *you* are so confident."

"That you are so confident, *lord King,*" Saldon admonished. When she did not trouble to look in his direction, he tucked back the corners of his mouth, hissed in an exasperated breath—and studied her with high interest.

She fears nothing, he mused. *Too bad she is not Velquen's daughter, to sit that throne of Empire!*

Valeron had chuckled. "Jheru: you are quite a woman. I have not seen another to compare, and we do grow *women* on Branarius, as we grow men. You slipped a blade into that Carmeian prison guard as if you'd been at the doing of such all your life. But—"

She shrugged, with attendant bounces. "He was a

traitor, one of Darcus Cannu's men. And—you needed help . . . lord King."

"Just the same, he was a countryman, and—"

"*Countryman!*" The word exploded from her. "I am no lily-sniffing *Carmeian!*"

"More like a fiend from the murkpit realm of Kroy," Saldon said, but this time when she jerked her head angrily his way she found that he was repaying her in kind by studiously looking elsewhere.

"Where are you from, Jheru?" Valeron asked.

She shrugged again, tossing a mane of hair black as space, and he jerked his eyes away. *Stop that!*" he snapped, gritting the words through clenched teeth. "Stop shrugging!"

"It—I really do . . . put discomfort on my lord?"

"You do. You are woman. What do you think I am, a 'lily-sniffing Carmeian'?"

Jheru rose and departed the control chamber.

"Peace at last," Saldon said.

"You are hard on her, Elder."

"I am a teacher. She has much to learn. She began by flaunting her ignorance. Then she began to listen. She learned. Hers is a good mind—and a high spirit. Better for us she were not aboard."

Valeron looked at him. "The why of that?"

"She attracts you. She is of the . . . construction you favor. She attracts, and distracts you. Lord King—pardon asked, but you have lain with her?"

"Saldon: I have not."

The more fool you, the Elder thought. *No wonder there's such nervousness with both of you! Both of you want that which you've not had.* He said, "I would do another question on you, lord King—again with apology."

"Heard; ask."

"And her mistress?"

"And her mistress—what?"

Saldon had his answer; the young warlord was far too casual and high of questioning brows. Valeron was well known to prefer utter wantons in the bedchamber; large women he called rock-cats.

"You make reply without words," Saldon said.

"And—is the Empress of the Seven Worlds a rock-cat?"

Valeron would not look at him. "You go far, Elder."

"Pardon asked, lord King."

"Granted without bias. So is silence in the matter."

The two men were silent, each thinking, the older with narrowed eyes fixed on the younger, who had gone visibly tight of face and back.

Then there was movement; Jheru returned, and the two men stared.

Her armor rustled and clinked link to link as she sat down; neither man asked of whom she had the leather winter-leggings or the undercoat or the loose coat of chain that covered her from collarbone to mid-thigh. Her aplomb was broken when she sat, without taking into consideration that the tail of her coat of steel links weighed enough to change her center of gravity. She did not lean back—she toppled, and had the seat been backless she'd have sprawled. Only just, Jheru preserved her frozen face.

"To answer," she said, and both men blinked. Neither smiled, though Valeron bent over his sword—long since perfectly clean and shining. "I was seven—so I am told—when I was brought to Carmeis from Ghulan. But there's little belief with me that I am of the Ghulani, either. Some said I had been brought to Ghulan from elsewhere still. No memory is with me of that, or of parents. I was seized by the police in Shalkh on Ghulan for street-fighting, sold for the fine, and put on a spacer with others bound for Carmeis. I was bought by a dealer and then by an agent of the emperor, with others, but . . . at the princess's request."

"Her Eminence asked for you?"

"She did, lord King. I have been her servant ever since."

Valeron was staring thoughtfully at her. "So far as you know you may be of Branarius, then."

"Hmp! I doubt *that!*"

At the sound of disdain, Saldon gave her a sharp look. She glared back, then growled low in her throat and gnashed her teeth, doglike, at him. Jheru laughed when the old man looked shocked. With a look of hauteur, Saldon turned back to the control console.

Once he felt her eyes leave him, he returned his thoughtful gaze to her. Coincidence, mayhap. But he had heard that growling sound before, and the dogs called muhmats existed only on Branarius.

When the silence grew too long to bear, she said, "My lord? Lord King?"

" 'Hmp! I doubt that,' " he imitated. "With me is the not-unpleasant thought of you strung up in the Sungoli fashion: arms high, feet only just touching the floor or ground, a separate slender cord of gut about each finger and thumb. I have seen men who have survived finger-hanging—without the use of their strangled digits. Others I have seen who did not survive. The bones of their rib cages protruded through the flesh, their tongues out . . . dead of a final inability of their lungs to labor on in such a position."

"*Gods*, my lord . . . it is thus you picture *me?*" Nor was she dissembling; she was genuinely shaken.

"None are so proud as the men—and women—of Branarius, *girl*. You hide behind your femaleness. A man taking that tone with those words you spoke would be dead—or worse."

Jheru's teeth dug deeply into the fullness of her lower lip. "Once before, lord King, Warlord of Branarius, have I told you: I have no disrespect for you, and I do not mean to offend. I . . ." She looked down, for her voice had quivered and she was as embarrassed by that as though she were of Branarius.

Valeron relented somewhat: "And your ultracivilized Carmeians call *me* an uncouth barbarian, partway because I say what comes to my mind without dissembling! You are a barbarian yourself, Jheru—and I congratulate you for it!"

She gave him a sidelong look from beneath dark brows, sidelong but not coquettish. "Perhaps," the mailclad slave of Carmeis said, "a barbarian warlord has need of such a woman about him."

Saldon, attempting to pretend great occupation with the ship's dials, snorted. And Valeron nodded.

"Aye. Suppose we end this life of slavery and return

you with us to Branarius when we go, Jheru. You will find life among my women both easy and pleasant . . ."

"Pardon asked, lord King—but is that not slavery as well?" Again her inner being seized her; tilted up her chin. "If I become a whore, I shall be paid for it!"

With an easy smile, Valeron imitated the High Counsellor's earlier remonstrance. "Careful with your talk, blowze!"

Jheru stared at him for a long moment with great nigh-black eyes. Then she rose, and clinked out of the cabin, notably stiff of back.

"So much," Valeron said, "for treating her as if she were not a slave."

"Very unwise, my boy. Nor can she ever *be* slave. It is not in her, any more than in you. Nevertheless, slaves are for serving, and for recreation, and it does not pay to treat them as equals. In this case, matters are worse—fear is with me that this girl has love for you."

"An un-Siense phrase from an Elder, Elder. But— love? You should have seen that one slip steel into the prison sentry."

"Those of us who are violent, my boy," Saldon said with the air of a man issuing a proclamation, "are violent in emotions as well."

"Now you are talking of me."

"As she was thinking of you—your life was endangered; she did death to keep death from you."

Valeron nodded at the banks of dials. "How long?"

Saldon peered at the instruments, which he had learned to read—somewhat. He studied the clock the Ancients had built into the console. "Just less than two hours. You intend no last-minute instructions?"

"I do. Although all plans hinge on what sort of reception we meet. I will go back and talk with the men before we disembark. Regardless of how we are met, I want no violence against any Maruthian. That I will have to tell my 'brother' Rankhnax . . . six or seven times. Just now—thought is on me."

"Far be it from me to interrupt such a process!"

Leaning back, Saldon gazed at the controls. The ship fled through empty space toward Maruthia. Saldon pondered, wished, thought. And suddenly Valeron was on his feet, the suddenness of the movement proclaiming a decision reached. The Elder looked his question at the other man.

"To answer your question of long ago—no, Saldon, she was but a kitten, and not even a kitten of the rock-cats."

Saldon sighed. He remembered the question; he'd asked about Aleysha's passion. He should not have put such a query. Yet the answer was to his liking; perhaps Aleysha and Empire needed Valeron. Surely, though, Branarius's need was greater.

"Too," Valeron said, "chainmail should not be worn aboard ship. Saldon: I go to see if we have not a stowaway aboard."

"What?" Saldon stared at the broad back of the warlord, who was leaving the control chamber.

"A rock-cat," Valeron called back, and left the cabin.

Saldon stared at the empty doorway. *It will do happiness on them both,* he thought. *Though I hope it leads not to unhappiness later—for either of them.*

To force his mind from this subject that he was hard put to remind himself was none of his business, the Elder returned his gaze to the controls, the dials of the rushing ship.

The Lord High Counselor to the Warlord of Branarius was an Elder, a Man of Siense, a man apart; his service to Siense was for life, though he no longer believed that Siense was the name of a god. He had spent many years—more than an average lifetime, already—and much money to recover some small portion of the lost knowledge of the mist-past.

Why did the ships go? Why and how did they "know" when to brake and land gently? No ship had ever been known to crash, even to behave erratically. And what in the name of the gods—*no, in the name of Siense not-god*—made the instrument panel light up? What was the riddle of the torchless, flameless, and nigh-heatless light, burning still after all these dead centuries?

Someday, Saldon thought, *we shall know*. He had not solved the problem, nor had anyone else, to his knowledge.

But someone would, sometime.

THIRTEEN

Horse and Automobile

DOWN into the atmosphere of Maruthia streaked the *Empress Aleysha*, bearing on its sleek sides the newly painted phoenix device of the ruler of Branarius. On the ground below, waiting men watched. Within the ship, Saldon patiently waited out the slight jerks, then bumps, before unfastening his belt. He stood as the console lights winked out. The Elder threw the lever; the ship had landed itself on Maruthia.

Saldon opened the rounded door and passed back into the vessel's main area. Seeing Valeron striding toward him, he stopped. *How much energy he expends in that long stride,* the Elder mused. *How much energy he possesses—and thank the gods for that!*

The new ruler of Branarius was unaccustomedly resplendent in gold-embroidered white tunic and polished black boots that rose to his knees. Purely ornamental spurs of wrought silver jingled, endangering his long red cloak and its lining of white satin. The conqueror looked strangely naked, Saldon thought, without his broad sword-belt and scabbard. The Elder stepped aside; the Warlord strode past.

"You think it wise to show yourself first, my boy? Perhaps we'd better allow one of the soldiers to step out, to see—"

"Some day I am going to order you to stop calling me 'my boy,' Saldon," Valeron said. "Be ready." It was his only reply.

He unlatched the port, pushed it open, stepped into the tiny room whose purpose none fully understood, and unlatched the outer port. He pushed it open. The big man squinted and turned his head as the bright sun from the coppery bowl of Maruthia's sky struck his eyes. After a moment he looked out upon the shipfield; acres of unrusted Ancient-material, gleaming mirror-like as mountain peaks in winter.

Then, with Saldon and Jheru at his heels, the ruler of the Barbarian World paced down the ramp.

A contingent of some thirty warriors in dust-colored tunics stiffly sat their horses at the foot of the catwalk. One of them dismounted and approached the foot of the ramp, gloved hand on pommel. His eyes swept from Valeron's swordless hip to his face; the tall Maruthian hardly had to look up. He and his men wore knee-high greaves of bronze-colored leather to match the aureate blaze of back-crested helms. Gloves and cloaks were russet.

"My lord King Valeron of Branarius?"

"Valeron, Warlord of all Branarius," Saldon said.

The officer glanced at him, nodded, and swung his head back to Valeron. "My lord, I am Prefect Graylon. Pardon asked, and by command of Lexton, King of all Maruthia, and in the name of the Council of Kings, my lord, you are under arrest."

Valeron nodded. "My sword is on the ship, Prefect; I do not surrender it. I would appreciate greatly—you said Graylon?—Prefect Graylon, if my men could be escorted off the ship and held elsewhere. There will be no trouble, assuming your men are polite; mine have their orders."

The prefect stared. "You . . . expected this?"

"Of course."

"Then . . . may I ask . . . uh, my lord Warlord, why you came here so openly and peacably?"

Valeron shrugged. "Branarius and Maruthia are not at war, Prefect Graylon."

Obviously that was hardly the answer the prefect had expected from this big brute he faced, the barbarous ruler of backward Branarius. As he stood considering, his face made it obvious that he had not been sure what to expect, and might indeed be afflicted by serious doubts as to the meaning of "barbarian." Yet the Maruthian showed less emotion than Valeron had thought he might and he respected the man for it.

"This is High Counselor Elder Saldon," Valeron

said, choosing each word—and enjoying himself immensely. The prefect would be obliged to report that Valeron was one of the most civilized men he had ever encountered . . . "And this is Jheru, of the court of the empress."

The beige-robed Elder bowed his head but faintly. Jheru, splendid in a saffron gown that covered her to the chin (and was slit from hem to the jewel high on her hip), repeated Saldon's silent acknowledgment— with a hauteur her mistress could have emulated to her credit, on state occasions.

"I shall have your men seen to properly, my lord. Um . . . won't you come with us?"

Valeron grinned at the Maruthian officer's discomfort only after he'd walked past Graylon to the waiting carriage. It was one of the marvelous shining self-propelling machines of the Ancients. Unlike those of the big shuttle-ships, the carriage's engines were long since inoperative. This one was drawn by four horses.

Valeron and his companions stepped in past opened doors; a Maruthian orderly closed them. Graylon rapped out orders to his men, wheeled his mount, ordered a wheel-about and forward. The carriage left the shipfield with Jheru sitting on the edge of her seat casting anxious glances this way and that. The horse-drawn vehicle rattled and creaked into the city. Graylon's men visibly strove not to cast anxious glances at the long smooth sheen of thigh and calf bared by the hip-high division of her gown.

"A revoltingly high humor is with you," Saldon said to his ruler, and Valeron turned his broad grin on him. "And my lord presented a grand imitation of a civilized man of reason."

Valeron bowed. "My thanks, Elder. I was thinking, Saldon, that Darcus Cannu likely has twice my intelligence and craft with him. And, that I am little more than a rock-cat: a collection of muscles and reflexes. Without you I mightn't be ruler at all. Poor Prefect Graylon expected just that: a thing of reflexes and muscle. Ready to do battle rather than submit to arrest. A savage! The poor fellow now tries to link that with my actions and words. Shock is with Graylon. I find that I like that—and now, Saldon, thought is with me of the kings, and Empire . . . what a surprise I have for *them*!"

Saldon and Jheru watched him as he sat, staring straight ahead, his smile unfading as he remembered again the mocking words of Darcus Cannu: "My lord *barbarian!*" Valeron muttered.

FOURTEEN
King and Barbarian

KING Lexton looked up from the letter to meet the questioning gaze of his chief minister. The king handed him the first letter, that bearing the imperial seal and addressed to Valeron.

"This was dictated and dispatched to Branarius several days before the emperor's death," Lexton said. "You will note it is addressed to Valeron, *Warlord of the Seventh World*, and *old friend*." His short white beard writhed as he spoke. Lexton's hair, which leaped back from his creased forehead in abundant, rippling waves, had been white since his twenty-and-ninth year, twenty years agone.

The chief minister began the letter aloud, allowed his voice to drop to a mumble as he read on, then: " 'There is another here, too, with anxiousness to see you,' " he read excitedly. " 'Let it be said that is one of the important matters we have to discuss.' Lord King! It is signed simply 'Velquen'!" He raised incredulous eyes to his ruler.

Without comment Lexton passed him the second letter. It too bore the imperial seal, and was addressed to King Lexton. His minister had watched the monarch break that seal. His brows rose still higher while his lips formed the words.

" 'Aleysha, Empress, to Lexton, King.' Apparently we enter a new era of formality, lord King. 'The Emperor has been murdered by DARCUS CANNU!' " the last two words exploded in an unministerial shout. Again the paunchy man stared with huge eyes at his ruler.

Lexton waved a hand for him to continue.

" '—by *Darcus Cannu,* who has bought off the Palatine Guard.' *Lord King!*"

"Read, Maron."

" 'The—the capital, the Empire, and the person of the Empress are in grave danger from this same traitor, Darcus Cannu.' " Again Maron stopped and looked up; again he met the unwavering eyes of his liege-lord; again he resumed reading, in a voice that was less than steady. " 'The bearer of this letter, the lord Valeron, now ruler of a united Branarius and therefore a member of Council of Kings, is acting as my personal legate, with powers plenipotentiary.' " He turned the letter over, glanced at it again, and then turned excited gaze on Lexton. "My *liege!*"

Lexton nodded his white head. "It is authentic. Both of them are—and I have not seen you so excited in years, Maron. Sentry! Have Prefect Gra— Ah, Prefect." Seeing Graylon entering, Lexton went on, "Conduct the Warlord of Branarius to me at once."

"Aye, sire. And the others? He is accompanied by an Elder he calls 'High Counselor,' and a Carmeian . . . woman he does not call Lady."

Lexton smiled. "Bring them also, and see that you do call her Lady, Prefect. He is no longer under arrest, and is to be treated according to his rank—which is equal to my own."

Prefect Graylon left the room with swift steps.

"Imperturbable sort," Lexton said of the departing officer, and his minister rolled his eyes; he had been thinking the same of the king. "Mark him. Graylon." Then, "Now, Maron. We have a few minutes . . ."

When Graylon returned, King Lexton was treated to the sight of the strangely grouped trio. The new ruler matched Graylon's one hundred ninety centimeters of height, and was broader of shoulder by the length of a hand. Between those broad shoulders his chest swelled to strain at the fabric of a white tunic. His polished jackboots clicked on tessellated tiles and Lexton noted that the big man wore spurs. At the new king's side walked an old man—an *old* man, Lexton realized—with a face like a sun-baked apple. He wore a straight-cut, unornamented robe of light brown girded with a knotted cord: the attire of an Elder of Siense.

Just behind them Lexton saw the young woman who
was not called Lady, all nut-brown and coppery against
the orange-and-gold of her garment; a short woman,
big of bone and well padded. The King of Maruthia
was neither so old nor so regal that he failed to note
well her sinuous walk and the pleasant jiggling that accompanied it, nor the long tawny legs that flashed
through the side-slits of her gown.

Not called Lady, indeed, the king mused; no, he'd
call her filcat, and he'd not mind testing her claws . . .

Graylon announced Valeron formally. His eyes
showed surprise when his monarch stood and descended
from his dais. The Branarian took the extended hand.

"Lord King."

"Lord King," Lexton echoed.

Valeron introduced his companions and the four of
them walked from the throne-room into a less formal
chamber furnished with a long council table and many
chairs, all backless. Over cups of chilled wine from the
vines of Nyor, the visitors outlined the situation.

". . . I realize there is little proof," Saldon added, "to
convince my lord king that the truth is with us and the
Carmeian ambassadors are lying . . . despite the letters
from Their Eminences. But—if they fail to break and
say truth when we confront them, surely a small amount
of persuasion will convince them of the blessed wisdom
of veracity."

"My lord king will note with what pretty words this
revered Elder suggests torture," Valeron said, and with
a smile he mitigated the words by raising a very large
hand to Saldon's bony shoulder. "At times it is difficult
to know which of us is in truth the 'barbarian' . . . I
make offer to submit to the persuasions he suggests, of
course."

Lexton returned the smile. "You will find, my lord
King Valeron, if you have not already, that 'barbarism'
is not confined to the world we have so long called the
Barbarian World. The fact that I have available the fa-
cilities of such suasion as the Elder mentions—and
that they have been made use of—makes the problem
of determining who is civilized and who is not even

more difficult. We Maruthians pride ourselves on our culture and our manners. The difference is that we have . . . refined our methods." The kings exchanged small smiles. "So, apparently," Lexton added, "has Darcus Cannu." He raised his voice. "Sentry!"

The young fellow popped in immediately and Lexton smiled. "So swift—worried about your king? And were this man an enemy, as he is not—do you think you could handle him? Make no answer—bring to us the emissaries from Carmeis, without a word to them of who is here."

The man saluted and departed; Lexton leaned back and smiled at Jheru, who almost-smiled in return. Though she'd spent nearly eleven years in the Imperial Palace, she had never been so awed and impressed; this time she sat *with* the mighty!

"Consider the highly cultured lover of art and fine food and dress, the gentleman priest-king, Narran ol-Shalkh Premn IV, of Ghulan," Lexton said, regarding the while a remarkable length of coppery leg distinguished by a curvature hardly believable. "On his world, torture has been refined to a point of high art . . . an art that men study, in schools. Yet Ghulan is a highly religious world, and a world of great beauty. It is hard to say which are greater, Ghulan's architects or its torture-masters. No, fear is with me that Branarius has no monopoly on what we are pleased—smugly—to call 'atavism' or 'barbarism,' my lords and lady."

Valeron sat back with a pleasant mien and calmly crossed leg as three Carmeian ambassadors were ushered into the council chamber. He knew none of them; none gave indication of recognizing him. New men of course, he mused; Darcus car Nu's sycophants, in richly embroidered and spendidly colorful attire.

"Gentlemen, we have the pleasure of entertaining honored guests," Lexton told them. "May I present Jheru, a lady of your own world, and Saldon, High Counselor of Branarius, and the lord Valer—"

He was interrupted. All three Carmeian faces sprang into expressions of shocked surprise. Two of the men managed slight smiles nonetheless—but the third, his face suddenly striving to match the ivory fur on his robe, broke.

"We're lost!" he cried, and at that moment they were.

Valeron had risen and was approaching them. As he neared, the third man snatched a dagger from the belt of his burgundy-hued robe and raised it, his face twisting in manic desperation. Up rushed the forearm, down it drove.

A huge copper-colored hand shot out to meet it. Valeron's fingers closed on the wrist of the knife-hand, squeezed, and his thumb touched his fingertips, overlapped them. For just an instant he looked with seeming calm into wide eyes. Then there was a crunching crack and the man screamed.

"Underhand with a knife," Valeron said. *"Always.* Never overhand . . . my lord."

Behind Valeron, Lexton was on his feet. He marveled. He had seen but the slightest tension of thews in the big barbarian's arm while he snapped the ambassador's wrist, with terrible ease. The fellow's eyes rolled up; Valeron released his wrist and stepped back. The Carmeian folded to the floor in a pain-induced faint.

The other two had remained still, resigned, knowing that their brief period of favor and expected power had ended. In likelihood they'd have done nothing, had not their companion made his attempt. Now one of them sprang forward, and he too plucked a dagger from his robe. Unaccountably, he lunged not at Valeron but at King Lexton . . .

A superlatively shaped leg snaked out to send him sprawling. The knife clattered across the floor. When the man stared up the length of the leg at Jheru's face, he felt the point of the sentry's sword at the back of his neck.

"Take these traitors belowstairs," Lexton ordered, and he stressed the last word. "See that they are well guarded. Send a detachment at once to occupy their ship. Oh, and by the gods! Free King Valeron's men!"

The sentry motioned the two emissaries of Darcus Cannu to the door.

"And send someone back for *this*," Lexton said, jerking his head at the sprawled man with the broken wrist. He turned, gave Valeron a look, and sank slowly back into his chair. The King of Maruthia refilled their goblets with Nyori wine.

"That is the closest I have been to death in thirteen years," he said, after he had drunk. "Since I stopped leading my men in person. Knowledge is with me that you and this young lady have saved my life, King Valeron." With a smile for Jheru, he lifted his goblet to her. "Quite a woman, incidentally, my lady. If you have not freed her, King Valeron, I shall grant Jheru her freedom so long as she remains on Maruthia."

She started, "How—"

"That band of paler flesh on your arm, Jheru. You've lately worn an armlet there—one you never took off."

"She is free on Branarius of course," Valeron said, and the girl of nineteen shot him a look. This was her first knowledge of that fact.

Lexton called for a scribe. "Prepare five copies of this letter for me at once. One is to be addressed to each of the other kings, and I want to hear ships leaving within the hour."

The scribe was prepared and poised.

"*Begins*. 'The Emperor has been murdered, as you have been told. Contrary to what you are being told, Valeron of Branarius is more than merely innocent. In my presence at this moment is the emissary and legate of Her Eminence the Empress Aleysha. He is Valeron, King called Warlord of Branarius, and he has just saved my very life from dagger-armed traitors claiming to be the Empress's ambassadors. They are not. The Carmeians recently arrived at your court are not. Beware! They are in the employ of the murderer of the Emperor Velquen. It is my advice that you imprison them immediately, say naught to anyone, release no craft to Carmeis, and proceed here at once. The Council of Kings must take immediate action: Her Eminence is, in her own words, in grave peril. The vulture flies darkly.' *Ends*. Just sign that 'Lexton,' and hurry, hurry now."

The King of Maruthia waited until the scribe had left, and then turned to Valeron. "That last phrase is the one we agreed upon to signal utmost urgency. I have never used it before."

FIFTEEN
Barbarian and Kings

JHERU looked down at the splendid gathering.

Lexton ni Nodh, thin and tall and white-maned, King of Maruthia, first world to join Carmeis after the Dark Time following the Wrath, long acknowledged chief of the Council of Kings. He was attired not as king but as Maruthian edgeman, in russet gloves and cloak over a tunic the color of dust, with leather greaves shining like bronze. Girt this king was with a sword-belt and scabbard, but it was empty; arms were not borne into such gatherings.

Vidul car Abar, black-bearded, sharp-eyed former general who had but two years past deposed the despotic Hajaar ni Nymsha, king of ever-restless Lavian; officially recognized now as a member of the Council of Kings—among whom he stood out starkly, in black tunic and high-gaitered buskins. Vidul wore no gloves; Vidul was minus three fingers.

Narran ol-Shalkh Premn IV, who had given up his wastrel existence on Carmeis to return home on the death of his father and become unquestioned monarch of Ghulan, shocking all by proving himself a brilliant administrator—and then by showing himself a religious fanatic; Ghulan's king alone wore baggy trousers beneath his knee-length tunic of scarlet.

Eshara II, short of hair and tightly corseted, over-cosmeticized King of Sid-Alors. So long as Empire had existed, there had been five kings. No such title as "queen" existed, for a ruling monarch. Like Eshara First before her, Eshara Second was called king. Over a gold-and-crimson-broidered white gown she wore a coral-hued shawl of the complicated lacework that was one of the most lucrative of Sid-Alori exports.

125

Finally there was the new lord, wary of eye, bare of arm, a hundred and ninety centimeters tall, brittle-speaking; the Warlord of infant Branarius—the man to whom the others had given ear these past two hours as though they had done so all their lives. He stood before them now, massive chest thrusting out the coat of linked chain he had donned to remind them that Empire was in a state of war. Buckled about his wrists were the black leather bracers of an edgeman; they flashed dully as he spoke, after the Branarian manner, with much use of his hands.

Only Nyor was not among them. Jallad car Ahmir, nineteen-year-old "Boy King" (since his twelfth year, and without a regent) of verdant Nyor, devoted seeker of knowledge—he was on Carmeis, and there was some nervousness about that fact.

Out of sight at the top of the stairway, Jheru looked down upon the glittering assemblage of power seated around Lexton's council table. Kings all of them; monarchs of worlds, not tribes or municipalities. And not all gray of hair, either, though Jallad was not among them and even his minister of state had been denied a seat at this Council of Kings. Their clothes were rich silks and velvets, furred and beaded and purfled and broidered, in hues that ranged the spectrum from white to black. Yet three among them wore military garb rather than finery; the warrior-king of Lavian, black eyes snapping above a black beard growing beneath black hair that was combed forward in square Lavi warrior-bangs above bushy black brows, wore his black tunic and buskins and shining black belt. Nor did he sit; Vidul was incapable of sitting long, and in the high places of other worlds there was more than a little worry over his ability long to reign. Here, he ranged the room while Valeron talked and others sat, and listened, and asked their questions. Vidul walked, leaned on table or windowsill or this chair or that, or sat briefly.

Valeron, too, stood. He bent over the table, casting those eyes Jheru thought so piercing and frightening at first one, then another of his new peers.

"Twelve days are gone since I left Carmeis—escaped furtively, as a fugitive accused of the highest murder. Furtively aided by the brave girl to whom we all now owe allegiance to the death. Two days hence she is to be married to Darcus Cannu. She hopes to postpone this marriage that is an obscenity. But it is obvious, my lords and lady kings, how ruthlessly clever this man is. He will do all he can to see the ceremony held as soon as possible." Valeron's eyes roved them. "The moment the Empress Aleysha becomes the bride of that murderous traitor, she is in constant danger of her very life."

He straightened, drawing their gazes up with him. "If there is any doubt with you that he will arrange her death, sooner or later, put it from you. Darcus car Nu wants the imperial crown. And he wants it as *his own*, unencumbered by a woman more powerful than he because she is Velquen's daughter. He will remove that encumbrance as soon as he feels it safe."

"That man has had the highest honors from us all," Eshara said. "What can be his motive for seeking the crown for his own—and at his age?"

"Perhaps," Narranol-Shalkh Premn said quietly, and they turned eyes upon him, "*empire*. I mean *Empire*. We are all kings; him—or her—we call emperor is little more than king over kings. He has little authority over our worlds; Carmeis has none. Perhaps Darcus Cannu, student of history and ambitious schemer, hopes to make Carmeis *ruler*, over *all*. We would become mere barons, owing far more than allegiance to the imperial person and world."

"With Palatine Guards on each of our worlds, imperial legates directing our actions?" That from Eshara.

Impassively, his voice absolutely without emotion, Vidul said, "He will die . . . horribly."

On the steps Jheru shuddered involuntarily. There had been several rumors as to the manner of death of the hated king deposed by Vidul, and several of his ministers as well. None of the stories had approached pleasantness. The Laviani were not known for their gentleness, and Vidul looked anything but tender and compassionate—or patient. A general who had seized the crown he wore could not be expected to become a diplomat overnight. Even the kings feared him.

Valeron bent forward over that gleaming table and again his naked fist crashed down with a solid thump. Almost without effort, without taking her gaze off him, Eshara caught her wine goblet as it tipped. Valeron's slitted eyes were blazing spots of terrible intensity and rage, peering from under his heavy brows.

"Darcus Cannu must be *stopped!* Darcus Cannu must *die!* The officers of *his* army, of the Palatine Guard, the fawning worms who are his emissaries . . . they must be punished; his co-conspirators must *die!* Our capital must be *freed!* Our ancient throne must be restored to the only person among the Seven Worlds with the right to sit upon it, Aleysha, Empress!"

Jheru shivered. Her heart thumped against her ribs as she watched them.

Jheru had seen many men and been known by several, not always by choice. After seeing this barbarian warlord with eyes at once fiery and chill, she knew that never before and never again, surely, would she see anyone deserving to be called man, unless a higher word were found for the Branarian. She had been more than fascinated, infatuated perhaps, with him even before he had come to her on the ship, after she had departed his and Saldon's company; "Out of that armor and what lies beneath, woman, so that I need not tear good chain links and my fingers in ripping it from you." Her haughtiness and cool gaze had lasted perhaps two seconds thereafter.

But what of those others down there? she wondered. *Do they feel it? Of do they fear him?* Did they see the giant beneath the mass of dark red hair and thick brows as a great man. the most forceful among them, among the Seven Worlds, a great leader who could not be gainsaid?—Or as a vicious, snarling animal, to be feared . . . or worse still, and the thought chilled her: to be used of necessity and then exterminated in fear?

Already all was not so united as they would have it appear, and pretend; every blueblood at that table distrusted and feared the farmer's son who had become a general and then a rebel and then revolutionary leader and—and then King of Lavian. Surely Vidul deliberately did mockery on them, with his somber garb.

He was stiffly afoot now, a quivering statue of black with pale knuckles where his hand clutched his forgotten goblet in a grip of anger. "Lavian's fighting men are ready to march on the traitors, behind Lavian's king!" he snapped. "To the death!"

"And Sid-Alors!" Eshara said, her eyes bright on Valeron, her voice harshly martial, deadly as only a woman's can be. She stood, tall and angular yet womanly, beside Vidul. "To the death!"

The others rose to pledge their forces to war against Darcus Cannu, and they were all gazing upon Valeron car Nadh of the Barbarian World.

"I give way to the premier edgeman and tactician among us," Lexton said. "The man who has held us with his words, and who has more personal reason than any of us to do battle with the plotters. With your approval, my lords and lady, I proffer command of the combined forces on King Valeron, the Empress's own legate."

Again they agreed loudly, even Vidul, whom Lexton had previously called the greatest warrior among them. As they subsided, the so-called Virgin King of Sid-Alors quietly smiled.

With her eyes on Valeron, Eshara said, "The armies of Sid-Alors will be overjoyed to be led by such a man . . . with the provision that I ride with you."

On the steps Jheru smiled a muliebrous smile. She strove to picture the old woman-king in armor, carrying a sword, bestriding a horse . . . yet that were easier than trying to visualize dour Narran in battle array! Valeron's shoulders, Jheru noticed now, seemed even wider, his chin even stronger, his chest even broader. King! The sixth king! King Valeron . . . it rang through her head, reverberating along the corridors of her mind . . .

As it did through his. He had spoken to them, harangued them. They had not only accepted him—they had made him their leader!

An impassioned speech had been written carefully by Saldon and drilled into Valeron's head, with the

changes he mandated. With Jheru as audience of one
he had rehearsed it again and again while they awaited
the arrival of the monarchs. Now she felt the blood
rush to her temples while she thrilled to his dynamic
winning of the rulers, none of whom he had ever seen
before, or they him; all of whom, excepting Vidul, had
been born to throne and scepter. Even Vidul, as
general under the king he'd deposed, had grown somewhat accustomed to high places and the society of
those who had been born or had risen to them.

Now Jheru knew that Valeron and Saldon had
planned for just this end.

Leader of the Council of Kings! The melodrama Saldon had written into the harangue had served its purpose, when powered by Valeron's magnetism. And the
young new ruler, carried away by his own emotions,
had departed from the speech, forgotten it, so that his
words came from his edgeman's heart.

And suddenly Jheru felt sadness. *He can have what
he wants. He will be Aleysha's. He will be emperor.
He would be a fool not to be—and so would those others below, not to push imperial scepter and throne and
seafoam green on him.*

"I am honored," he was telling them, like a courtier
and yet with a simplicity that stemmed partly from his
inability to think of better words, partly from an attack
of shyness now the adrenalin had worn off—and partly,
in truth, from a barbarian's contempt for a string of
pretty words. "I accept your trust with pride. Now let
us sit down and make our plans; we have little time."

As they resumed their seats, he glanced over their
heads at the womanish shadow high on the steps. She
sat hugging her knees. He flashed a smile, and Jheru
felt a sudden dizziness.

Then the slitted jungle eyes snapped down, swung
their slashing gaze about over the gathered royalty with
corruscating fury.

"Darcus Cannu has provided us with the means to
take him without war," Valeron said, and Vidul gave
him a strange look. "He sent ambassadors to each of
your worlds. We have their ships, five spacers bearing
the imperial coat-of-arms. Those ships will take us to

Carmeis, all of us, and those ships will land without arousing suspicion or any attention beyond normal. The Carmeians at the shipfields know who is aboard—except that they will be wrong. Each ship will be filled with fighting men—and each will be followed closely by another, until all of us have landed on Carmeis—with a force of edgemen . . . and totally unreported at the palace!"

Three kings, a queen-called-king, and a slavegirl called lady listened as a master militarist outlined strategy. From time to time one of them nodded, or another interrupted him with a question of the what-if variety. Vidul, who had gained his crown through bloody martial action based on preplanned strategy, gazed at the Branarian. The black Lavi eyes reflected the automatic respect of one soldier-tactician for another. Eshara caught Lexton's glance and nodded with a faint smile. Narran stared at the barbarian newcomer with open admiration.

Jheru never took her gaze from him. His swift-moving hands, his thick, tapping fingers, his mighty fist as it emphasized his points, his hand lifting to push impatiently at the darkly ruddy hair that insisted on sliding over his forehead; she watched it all.

When he finished, they rose to drink to him and their success, and he turned back their hail, directing it with surprising grace to the empress. Jheru rose slowly, turned, and scuttled.

He strode into her room to find her waiting in darkness. "Where's Saldon?"

"Asleep, my lord King."

"Hell he is! Confident devil—and why are you not asleep?"

"I have been listening, lord King."

He grinned, and the grin was boyish as the long strain slipped away. He astonished her by asking, "How did I do?"

"You were wonderful, my lord."

"Time you ceased my-lording me, Jheru. I said you were free—I meant it. I had decided before Lexton made mention. We will make it official if need be, when this is over. On Branarius *and* Carmeis."

"You would dare free a slave of the empress herself?"

Without hesitation he said, "I would. I will."

Before he could move or say more, her arms were around his neck and her body was pressed hard and aching against his. Her lips yearned up to his.

"You *are* my lord," she told him, from the throat. "I'll not be free of you."

Nor was she, for hours, and never had Jheru been so fiercely used—or delighted so in it.

SIXTEEN

Scepters and Swords

PREFECTOR Abdu, in charge of the shipfield a kilometer outside Carmeis City, had never witnessed such frenzied action. A ship bearing the imperial insignia had come whistling down to berth and soon a man in the tan uniform of Maruthia was sprinting across the field to Abdu's tower.

"Prefect Graylon, Royal Army of Maruthia," he had barked, panting, before the door had time to close behind him. "That ship bears my lord King Lexton. Five others will arrrive at intervals of approximately fifteen minutes. They bear the other kings. You—"

"King Lex—the *other* kings! All of them? The *kings?*"

"—must clear each ship out of the way for the next one to set down."

Prefector Abdu swallowed. Never had he been faced with such a mass landing, much less the Five Kings—all at once! He had seen but one of them in the four years he had held post at the field—unless one counted that Branarian murderer. In his excitement he seized on certain knowledge:

"But—King Jallad is already here, there can't be—"

"Prefector! The lord King of Maruthia awaits. Others come. The last ship bears that boy Jallad's high minister—we *know* he's here, man!"

"I—aye." Abdu's lips twitched in a smile; two edgemen shared the calling of young Jallad "boy," and Abdu was made more comfortable thereby. His brain began to clear, to function. He reached for the loudhorn on his desk. "I must send a courier to the palace, at once."

"Pardon asked, Prefector, but I have taken the

liberty of sending a runner to the palace," Graylon lied, with easy smoothness. "Thought was with me of your need to concentrate on each landing and the directing of your men."

"*Thank you!*" Abdu said, with fervor, and he forgot his courier.

The Carmeian commander swung to the window, lifted the loud-horn, and commenced bawling echoic orders to the men on the field. Graylon watched, a bit amused—and not without respect. The Carmeian handled the situation admirably, if not with consummate calmness. Within eight minutes, the spacer from Maruthia was out of the landing slot and on a ramp.

His men returned to the landing slot just as the second big craft came whistling down onto the glassily gleaming plain. Instantly men swarmed over it like the busiest of ants.

When the sixth vessel was safely down, Abdu mopped his brow and bit his lip. He shot a glance down at the Maruthian prefect—Graylon, was that it? Now what? There was nothing in the Book of Protocol, drawn up years previously by Darcus Cannu himself, to cover this unprecedented situation. Six ships bearing emissaries of the new regime had departed for the other world—and now all returned at once, each bringing a king, presumably for a mass declaration of sympathy—and fealty to the girlish new empress. But— what to do now?

At least that Graylon fellow had helped out by sending a messenger to the palace. Here he came now, returning, ascending to the tower with two of his own men in their rather dull uniforms.

"Prefector: my respects and congratulations. You've done a marvelous job," Graylon told him as he entered the tower followed by the two soldiers. "It is now my painful duty to advise you that this field is under control and command of the Six Kings. Please remain here with these men; you are relieved, sir."

Abdu stared. Now he realized—the lying offworlder hadn't notified the palace at all. He'd been tricked; trapped; he'd helped land . . . what? A . . . an *invasion?* Incredible, unthinkable! But—what was it then? He glanced down. More Maruthian edgemen swarmed over the field. An *invasion?* The . . . the *kings?*

"What— I do not understand, Prefect. What . . . is this?"

"My men will enlighten you, sir. I note that you are unarmed, and they have instructions to respect your rank and position. Unfortunately time is not with me. Until we determine who is guilty here and who is not, the charge against you is treason."

"Treason!"

With a bow, Graylon turned and descended to the field. Abdu stared at his two guards. Slowly he sank into the chair at this desk. He glanced at the loudspeaking horn; at the two granite-faced soldiers from offworld; decided to forego heroism. His mind churned. And then at last that one strangest of all Graylon's words exploded like a flare in his brain.

"Six kings!"

His small shipfield force, meanwhile, had been taken completely by surprise. Most of them were stevedores, naturally unarmed, and they surrendered at once. The little armed force of twenty soldiers, here in the main for ceremonial purpose and with never-blooded swords, took one look at the other ships disgorging their helmeted edgemen—and quickly followed the example set by the workers.

The shipfield of Carmeis, Graylon reported to the commander of the Council forces, had been taken without a sword's being raised in its defense.

"Very good," Valeron said, and he smiled. "Very, very good, Prefect. Disarm them and hold them in that building, over there. And let us keep memory with us of this, Graylon: *This is monstrous!* New security measures must be set up for this most important of fields; we should never have been allowed to accomplish this with such ease!" He swung an arm in a gesture that encompassed the captives. "All these men should have died before laying down their arms! This is Carmeis, this is the heart of Empire! Think on it, Graylon, and note well this place; we must rework all, install absolute security, and with the proper men. Do you want command of the defense of Carmeis—of Empire?"

Leaving the Maruthian to ponder that in some astonishment, Valeron turned to his own aide. Graylon stood still, a struggle to maintain his imperturbability.

"Burgon," Valeron said, "inform the lord kings that the field is ours without a fight. Get them all down here and supervise an orderly—and fast—formation of the troops."

Burgon saluted and spun to his adjutants.

Aside from the royalty of four of the five worlds—and Branarius—the ships bore a combined force of two thousand men. They trotted down the ramps, carefully out of step, to form quickly on the field. A dull-eyed Prefector Abdu looked down on serried ranks of gleaming armor and nodding crests and fluttering cloaks of six different hues; even in the absence of its king, Nyor too had sent its contingent of edgemen.

Thumbs in weapon-belt above wide-planted feet, Valeron watched the landing and forming up of his force. He glanced up to see King Lexton, his snowy hair lifting in the slight breeze, smiling and nodding as he surveyed the scene. The Maruthian ruler was flanked by Saldon and Jheru, whose eyes were on Valeron. She glanced quickly away when he looked her way. She had been passing quiet on the voyage and had made herself as unobtrusive as possible.

At first Valeron had given her actions little thought, assuming she was overawed by the concentration of royalty and the monumental implications of their mission. So was he, when he was not busy with the planning and replanning of its carrying out. Then he realized that she had been weeping, that she'd gone inexplicably and uncharacteristically mute in his presence—which she seemed too to avoid. That night in dayless space he had lain long awake, pondering the future.

Jheru was a woman in love, Saldon had said. (*In love?* Valeron thought. *In love?—she wants me. Again.*)

She is also still a slave, he reminded himself, *and a dangerous in-fighter*.

And—what do I want?

He remembered Velquen's letter; remembered a beautiful young woman: Jheru's age and yet younger than Jheru. A seven-studded crown on her head and the pendant of Empire between the wide-separated little breasts that had later been naked in his hands. *Her father chose me. She chose me. I was her first.*

He remembered the long, long hall, watched over by its twin lines of columns of silent marble women. And he remembered the immense chair of priceless plast.

The throne of Empire.

The throne of the emperor. The seat of the man who became Aleysha's husband, for this was a culture just up from the dark, a male culture. The man who sat that highest of seats would father the children who would rule after him ... a long, long step for a barbarian orphaned and raised by savages!

"In a few days," Saldon had said, "assuming our success, the hand of Aleysha and the throne of Empire will be yours for the taking."

And Branarius? Who will mold Branarius into a power while I am on Carmeis?

Who? Saldon? Dernon car Kend, who now acted as regent in his presumably temporary absence? Burgon? And—*would* Aleysha's husband be emperor? Would he *rule?*—or must he be an extraneous consort, and edgeman ringed about with clever, educated courtiers and bogged down in protocol and sham and economics and plans for the next reception?

For the matter of that—and both Jheru and Saldon, separately and in manner different, had posed this question—would the kings *allow* such a union? Or would they fear him too much, want him far away on Branarious as soon as his usefulness in this immediate exigency was needed?

"The strongest hand in Empire," Vidul had said quietly, dark eyes steady on Valeron's, "should wield the scepter and the power that rules Empire."

"And ... will he someday have to face Vidul over edge of shield?" Valeron asked, with the complete openness of one edgeman to another.

"You assume I spoke of you."

Valeron nodded. "So I assumed, my lord King Vidul."

"I suppose that . . . it is not impossible that . . . someone might dispute you for the throne of Empire."

Valeron sighed. "And die thereby, and rend Empire the while. We two alone of all the others are edgemen, Vidul. We two alone among the kings have carved out our own kingdoms, crowned our own heads. We two have much to do, each of us on his own world. Must we dispute another throne, and rock all thrones and seven worlds in the doing of it?"

"No. There is no 'must' with us, Valeron of Branarius. But . . . who knows?"

Jheru had heard that, Valeron knew. Jheru had heard Saldon, too. And Jheru had heard Lexton tell Eshara that it boded only good for Empire that Velquen's choice for his daughter's spouse coincided with her own, and that that man was one who would be strongest in the throne in generations. And she had heard Eshara ask, though it was not really a question at all, "Too strong?", and Jheru had told Valeron of those words.

So many facets of this jewel that was Empire and this problem concerning it! So many questions!

And I—what do I want?

Aleysha would not be enough; his own dalliance with her was sufficient to put sureness with him of that. Well and well; an emperor had his privileges, as did any ruler, any strong man who dominated his woman. But—did he covet that greatest of all great thrones?

How could he not? Son of a fallen warrior and a murdered mother; foster-son of Sungoli savages; never treated by them as equal nor later by his own kind; called "My lord *Barbarian*" by the murderer of the emperor . . . *how could I not covet that woman, that slim body, and that swollen throne of swollen authority and power? I had to show the Sungoli . . . I had to show my own. . . I showed all Branarius. And oh, would an Emperor Valeron show them all—all, all that there are seven worlds!*

Saldon has said it. I must prove my own worthiness to my own self, day after day. Though I like not the

*words, they are true. And I must prove my worthiness
too to others; the Sungoli-reared barbarian from the
Barbarian World is as good as any—better! And he
can be just as civilized, too!*

Can't he?

What do I want?

A hand on Valeron's arm tore him from the mental
torture-chamber in which he had languished for days.
It was Lexton. Eshara and the other kings, in colorful
martial array, stood grouped about him. The white
plumes of Eshara's golden casque nodded in direct contrast with the black horsehair crest of the black-helmed
man beside her; dark and ever-sinister Vidul.

Valeron and the King of Maruthia had long since
dropped the time-consuming formality of the prefaces
"my lord" and "lord King." They looked at each other
as two men, each with respect with him for the other.

"Lexton: I'm leaving nearly all the force here under
your Prefect Graylon. We will take only a small detachment into the city. I'll get into the Carmeian uniform and act as escort; fifteen of my men are already
commandeering Carmeian garb."

Lexton nodded. Beside him stood level-eyed Narran ol-Shalkh Premn, the ornate pommel of a broadsword protruding from the silver-chased sheath on his
left hip. A ceremonial and entirely serviceable dagger
was strapped in the manner of his people to his left
forearm, hilt down. Another rode his hip.

"Think you we will have trouble gaining the
palace?" he asked. His face was without seeming apprehension, smooth and neatly bearded beneath an ornate
gryphon-crested helmet of gleaming silver over steel.

Valeron shook his head. "We shouldn't, lord King,
assuming you mean reaching it. Why should we? No
one is expecting us. No one *ever* expects invasion, and
certainly not by the kings themsel—ourselves. There is
far, far too little security here. It is for us to remember,
and correct later."

"And *at* the palace, lord King Valeron?" Eshara
asked.

The tall woman wore a fur-trimmed robe of a bright
apricot color, falling from a high neck to blouse over

her broad belt and thence to her ankles. It was slit from hem to hip and wide of armholes; beneath it her big-boned frame was encased in padded chainmail. She wore sword and dagger.

"I've no more toleration with me of 'lord King' and 'my lord' from any of you," Valeron told her. "As to the question—we will see. Once inside the palace we'll deploy our men and proceed straight to the Hall of a Hundred Women. We must assume that the Palatine Guard are his to a man, until we—and they—prove otherwise. Surely the sight of all of you should end their resistance. If it does not, Eshara—well, that's why you wear mail this day!" He did not do insult on her again by suggesting—as he had before—that she remain here on the field. "The rest of the soldiers and certainly the people have no knowledge of what has befallen *their* emperor, of what takes place in *their* palace."

"Darcus Cannu?" That from fat Narran, whose mail-coat must have taken nigh twice the usual time to link together.

"We will simply inform Darcus car Nu that he is under arrest," Valeron said.

Vidul raised tenebrous brows at him; the others nodded. For a moment Valeron looked about at them, meeting their eyes one by one. *The kings! The Council of Kings—and they listen to me, and I lead them! And . . . shall I lead you the rest of my life, my noble and kingly lords and lady?*

Premature, Valeron told himself; his life might well be an hour or hours away from its end! He turned from them and hurried to the barracks to find and don a Carmeian uniform. Finding a helmet with the dot-within-a-circle that was a captain's insignia, he forced it over his hair—and tucked-up Warrior's Knot. He strode back to the waiting kings clasping a white Carmeian cloak over a cerulean Carmeian tunic.

They stared at him, four monarchs dressed for war.

"My lady . . . my lords . . . let us ride."

The Five Kings mounted, and they rode.

Valeron and his fifteen disguised Branarians spurred ahead. Just behind came four close-bunched riders; the royalty of Empire, not without some wonder as to the sixth of their number, who had by now been two weeks in Carmeis City. Seventy men, fourteen from each of their worlds and from Jallad's as well, followed.

"Get that gate open," Valeron ordered even before they reached the heavy gates that opened into the city. "I escort the Four Kings!"

The eyes of the gate-officer went wide; so *this* was the meaning of the sudden influx of down-screaming ships! With a bow, he turned to snap a quick command, then swung back to Valeron.

"Has the palace been informed of their arrival, Captain?"

A courier in quest of information had come galloping from the city out to the shipfield to inquire about the multiple landing; he was now incarcerated with the others. Valeron nodded.

"Of course. We are expected. You should have received orders concerning us."

The Carmeian nodded without betraying to the mass of royalty that even the imperial guardsmen could be inefficient.

"Captain . . . their *attire*—I—I recognize two of my lord Kings, b-but—all are armored—and armed!"

Valeron sighed. "Another word and I'll have your name on a list you won't like, Sergeant. Of course they are so attired—think you the Five Kings of Empire pledge fealty to the empress with wooden swords?"

"Nosir. Sorrysir. M'lord Kings—uh, and m'lady King—uh . . ."

The gates were opened; Valeron spurred; the sergeant was spared self-extrication from his own verbal quicksand. He and his men watched in voiceless awe while the flashing procession streamed through the gate and into the capital. The last fourteen mounted escort of the party turned and rode back—trousered men of Ghulan.

"How many men are assigned to this gate?"

The sergeant had not the faintest notion as to the rank of his bearded questioner. Who could know about men who went about in baggy breeches rather than mannishly bare legs under kilts? He recognized the clothing with an inward smile as Ghulani, but knew nothing of the rank-symbols of that fanatically religious world.

"We five," he said, and added "sir" to be safe.

At that moment the Carmeians realized that they had been quietly surrounded.

One man made a grab for the pike he'd left leaning against the high wall. One of the Ghulani leaned from his saddle and with a *chunk* like a dropped watermelon sent the poor fellow's head arolling.

The sergeant snatched out his sword. He sprang at the mounted offworlders with their pointed beards and curved swords and one of those strange blades split his chest from neck to navel while another chopped into his upper arm.

The other three Carmeians surrendered.

The men from Ghulan swung open the gate. One of their number galloped back toward the field, while his companions held the former guards at swordpoint.

"The gate to the Imperial City should be guarded by Ghulani," one captor said, the black spade of his beard writhing as he spoke. "No Ghulanyi surrenders to invaders!"

The maneuver had been planned in advance; in an astonishingly short time the rider came bucketing back, followed by the fifty others Valeron had mandated.

"Forty of you on the other side of the gate, with the prisoners. Ten on the walls. No one enters or leaves by this gate. No one. Take these bodies out with you."

Then the man from Ghulan turned and led his little contingent after the kings. With them went a fifteenth warrior, in the uniform and armor of Ghulan.

The three Carmeian prisoners stared.

SEVENTEEN
Swórds and Kings

DARCUS Cannu, Valeron had reasoned, would have been stupid to advise more men than necessary of his plans. A few officers; perhaps a few men assigned to palace duty—and frozen there . . . these would have traded him their loyalty and their silence for Carmeian coin and promises.

Valeron grunted a barbarous malediction when he saw the detachment of Palatine Guardsmen drilling in the courtyard beside the palace, although he supposed that in all likelihood these men were not privy to Darcus Cannu's plans. The likelihood was that they were here *just in case*—and were wondering why in the name of Siense they were tramping around under the unappreciative eye of a nervous gardener. After regarding them in silence for a time, Valeron turned to one of his disguised Branarians.

"Wait you here. If there's trouble, get back and start our force on its way here—at the fast-trot. And tell Saldon and Jheru to depart for Branarius, no matter what. The gate is ours, by now."

With a nod, the man reined back and around. He paced his mount past a man with low-pulled helmet and bowed head—and winked; Rankhnax the Sungol was about as unobtrusive as a heifer in a greenhouse.

Soldiers respected rank, Valeron knew; this began the first day of a bound-edgeman's training. If a man wore one's uniform and his rank exceeded one's own, one just did not demand his identity—save in the field—unless one relished castigation, restriction, or worse. Nor was there reason for passwords or picket lines at the Imperial Palace. Valeron was well aware that soldiers came and went at will, usually someone

143

else's will. Civilians were questioned only if they were not carrying orders or invitations or a palace pass. These thoughts occupied his mind as his procession came alongside the long flight of steps leading up to the palace doors.

A sergeant and two halberdiers came down to meet them. They saluted Valeron's uniform.

He waved a hand as a return salute and said with deliberate urgency, "Sergeant, these are the other four kings, come to join my lord King Jallad in pledging fealty to the empress. These others are their retainers. Orders are with you to admit them at once?"

The sergeant licked his lips, wide-eyed. Did the empress's sergeant genuflect to the kings—the *Kings?* "Why—n-nosir . . . I've been told nothing—"

Valeron cursed one of the colorless oaths of the civilized worlds. "Damn that runner," he added. "Who in Kroy's name is Officer of the Day?"

"C-Captain Tarku, sir."

"I might have known! Well, *I'll* answer to *him*. . . or he to me! Sergeant, I am taking this party in. My responsibility."

The sergeant saluted happily. "Yes, *sir!*" The difficult matter had been taken out of his hands.

Valeron led the other kings and their tiny "invasion force" into the Imperial Palace. A dozen or so of his little force of edgemen hung about the palace doors, chatting with the sergeant and his men . . . and ready to carve them into bits if the situation demanded.

"Guard!"

"*Sir!*"

"Where is Her Eminence the Empress?"

"In the throne-room, *sir!*"

"And the Prime Minister?"

"With her, *sir!*"

"Guardsmen, I do appreciate your swiftness and decisiveness. Here: Captain Tarku has been relieved of command—permanently. I want all palace guards in the council room *at once*. You can handle that, Guardsman?"

"Yes, *sir!*"

"A good man, Captain," Lexton said. "Guardsman, I am Lexton, King of Maruthia. Your name, please?"

The astonished guardsman gave it, was smiled upon and bade be on his mission, and stepped hurriedly back to snap a salute. About-facing beautifully, he *ran* up the corridor. Valeron watched him relay the order to each man he passed. Also watching at Valeron's side, Vidul grinned and darkly shook his head.

"I did not find the seizing of power on Lavian *quite* so simple," he muttered into Valeron's ear.

Eshara was smiling. It was the "barbarian's" imperious assurance that did it, she mused, and then corrected herself: It was *King Valeron's* imperious assurance!

"Burgon," King Valeron muttered, "when those prissy fellows are in the council chamber, your work begins. Advise them that they have been called thither by the prime minister, who will be with them shortly. Then close the doors on them, take the Maruthians, and *hold the Carmeians inside*." Valeron swung to Vidul without waiting even for Burgon's nod. "I want your men and mine in the throne-room, Vidul. The janizaries and whatever Palatine Guardsmen are in there are under separate command, and we may have to deal with them." He touched his sword-hilt. "If our men aren't the best among us, you and I should be whipped."

Vidul nodded and his beard writhed with his sinister smile.

It was the jet blackness of his hair and beard and the way it crowded his face, Valeron mused, along with Vidul's unhandsomeness; the man couldn't help but look menacing!

Burgon and the Branarians, each in the uniform of a guardsman now shivering back at the field, legged it down the corridor to the big council chamber. The edgemen from Maruthia followed; Burgon's men would return once the Carmeians were mured up in the council chamber. Ten Laviani and the trousered men of Ghulan followed Valeron and the Council of Kings up the vaulted palace corridor toward the Hall of a Hundred Women. The Sid-Alori wandered about the broad corridor, ostensibly rubbernecking as might be expected of first-time offworld visitors to the capital of Empire. The Nyori of King Jallad car Ahmir remained in the antechamber to the throne-room. They were ready to deal with the stony-faced guards if necessary.

It had not occurred to them that Valeron and the other kings could not be sure of Jallad, presumably still here after a tenday and more; the Nyori, then, were better separated from those they might well turn on in the name of their youthful liege-lord . . .

The head of the empress snapped up when one of her guardsmen announced the presence in the antechamber of fourteen Maruthian ambassadors. To her left, Jallad of Nyor lifted his brows and gazed the length of the great hall at the doors. Aleysha's eyes widened, then narrowed quickly as she caught control of herself. Valeron had gone to Branarius, and from there she knew he'd have headed straight to Maruthia. She turned innocent gaze on her prime minister.

Darcus was frowning.

"Is knowledge of aught of this with you, Darcus?" she asked, hoping the *slam-slamm*ing of her heart was not visible beneath its satin-and-lace covering.

"Nothing. And we should have been apprised of their arrival immediately they stepped off their ship, by a courier from the field. Perhaps we had best—"

"Send them in at once," Aleysha said, in a clear voice.

The guard bowed and returned the long length of the carpet to the doors. Darcus Cannu swung to her, his voice low and hissing.

"Maruthian ambassadors? Maruthia? What in Kroy's name can *they* want?"

"Prime Minister—your language! I'm certain I can't say, Darcus," she said, shaking her head. "Perhaps they have word of Valeron? But more likely King Lexton sent them with a formal declaration of allegiance. I have expected *some* acknowledgment from the kings."

Jallad, tall and slim and smooth-faced, remained silent. As Darcus Cannu turned his attention to the doors again, Aleysha glanced at the youngest king. Their eyes met. King Jallad wore a decorated white

tunic, a dress-belt sewn with cloth-of-gold, and a ceremonial sword in a highly ornamented scabbard. Another hilt protruded from the sheath on his right hip, a
strange sheath, short and rounded; Jallad car Ahmir,
so-called Boy King of Nyor, apparently carried a most
unusual dagger.

All three at the throne watched, silent and waiting,
while an unusually tall, helmeted Palatine captain entered. Behind him were others . . . The prime minister
recognized King Lexton . . . King Eshara . . .

"The kings!" he gasped, and his eyes snapped wide.
"The Five Kings!"

"No no, Prime Minister," Jallad said quietly. "I am
here."

Behind the large party of royalty and retainers, the
Laviani edgemen barred the doors.

"Darcus Cannu was right," Valeron said, coming
with long strides down the carpet to the dais. "Five
Kings we are, come to restore the empire to the daughter of its emperor."

Darcus Cannu's face went the paler. "Who—"

The clanging to the floor of the tall captain's helmet
interrupted him, and answered his question.

"—*Valeron!*"

"Aye, Prime Minister. The Sixth King . . . 'my lord
barbarian,' in your last words to me. Your proclama-
tions state that the Emperor Velquen's murderer will be
hanged. We agree, Darcus car Nu. And we are here to
do the hanging."

A movement tugged Valeron's gaze momentarily
from the writhing face of Darcus Cannu. As he looked
into the angular features of slim Jallad—Lexton had
murmured that it was he, there at Aleysha's left, as they
approached—the Branarian saw the King of Nyor nod,
closing both eyes. Valeron's gaze swept to Aleysha.

"He knows," she said, and Valeron assumed that Jallad was with them.

But not Darcus Cannu. In the throne-room were two
secretaries, three servants, and, in the arcade beyond
the caryatids, no less than twenty Palatines. The prime
minister leveled a quivering forefinger at Valeron and
spat one word:

"Guards!"

The excellent voice of King Lexton boomed.

"Soldiers of Empire! I am Lexton, King of Maruthia. We are all here; the Council of Kings. We have named King Valeron our commander. On that throne sits your liege and our empress. Beside her stands—her father's murderer, Darcus Cannu, *traitor*. We are here to take him. The palace is surrounded—and your own cohorts are locked up in the council chamber."

Lexton's gaze swung over them, men frozen into frozen immobility, shocked by his eyes and his words. Before one of them could consider the total impossibility of the palace's being surrounded without their knowledge, Lexton spoke the more.

"Decide now, soldiers of Empire. Will you obey this man, this highest traitor, this *murderer*, or will you throw down your swords and await judgment . . . until we decide who here is guilty of treason?"

They hesitated—and looked now to their commander. When he saw this, Darcus Cannu swung his arm—to point at the Palatine Prefect.

"You are wrong, my lord King! He did it: Prefect Alerku guided the dagger that went into the emperor's back! Alerku! There is but one chance now—your sword!"

An aging woman's voice tore at Darcus Cannu like a dry, slashing wind. "You could not know this," Eshara said, "unless *you* gave Alerku the order to kill Velquen, Darcus car Nu!"

Valeron was right; these palace guardsmen were Cannu's men. As Alerku's hand went to his hilt, they drew swords and came rushing forward. The Council force drew to meet them. Steel clashed and rang. A man screamed. Swinging his blade up to send another spinning away, Valeron saw Vidul charge past. The King of Lavian slammed a hip into one man's body so that he went staggering back, starting to fall, at the same time as Vidul stabbed a second through the left side. He had the blade out so swiftly that the fellow was still erect before Vidul was hewing away a vicious cut at his head.

Beside Valeron, Lexton was happy to have an oncoming sword deflected by the Branarian's blade so that it missed the other monarch's belly. On the backswing Valeron opened that Palatine's inner left thigh. Valeron's own left leg was leaping out, to drive his foot into the crotch of a third guardsman—but that man was slain before he could moan and grab himself—slain by another Carmeian!

The Warlord of Branarius grinned an ugly wolf's grin. They were split, then. *Good!* Some were not traitors—or relented at the prospect of fighting the very kings themselves. But both secretaries and one of the slaves—now two—had seized weapons to join the Carmeian soldiers against the Council force.

Valeron glimpsed a trousered Ghulanyi spring to meet the armed slavegirl— No! The short warrior with the big chest was no Ghulanyi, and the chest was not a man's barrel, either. It was Jheru! Armed, armored, wearing the uniform of some edgeman of Ghulan she had charmed—best not to ask how—in order to join Valeron here despite his orders. Angrily he grasped a pike-butt and slammed it back into the wielder's belly —or crotch, it mattered not which; the blow ruptured entrails—before making his way to Jheru.

She did not need him, he saw. A silvery sweep of her blade sent the dagger flying from the hand of the slavegirl, who with a shriek dropped to her knees to implore her fellow slave. Contemptuously, almost in passing, Jheru cracked her in the jaw with a steel-bossed bracer. The slave fell and was stepped on by a guardsman, who fell—and lost an outflung arm to Jheru's sword. Wheeling, she chopped at the back of the man who had just crossed blades ringingly with King Eshara. He turned; while he was stupidly raising his sword for a stroke, Jheru stuck him in the belly—at the same time as Eshara's double-edged Sid-Alori blade bit more than halfway through his neck.

Alerku did not fight. Still staring openmouthed at the prime minister, he reached across his slim belly to yank out his sword.

"NO!" the Palatine Prefect shouted, and hurled the weapon clanging and crashing to the floor. "NO! These are the KINGS! This is the Hall of a Hundred Women —the Hall of Empire! No! Stop: I order you to throw down your weapons at once! We *cannot* fight the Kings!"

A hush swept like a dark cloak over that milling crowd of combatants. Eyes stared. Then there was the clash and rattling clangor of steel on tile . . . another. A fourth sword was flung down, and others still. The Palatine Guardsmen of Prefect Alerku stood disarmed —self-disarmed.

Eyes. Eyes, the eyes of Branarius and Ghulan and Carmeis and Sid-Alors and Nyor and Maruthia and Lavian; all swept their gazes toward the throne. They fastened themselves on the thin man there in his purple robe.

The prime minister looked about at them, his head jerking, his eyes narrowed and ablaze. He was a man alone.

A voice spoke. "Darcus Cannu: in the name of the Six Kings, you are under arrest for treason and murder."

The voice was that of Vidul car Abar of Lavian.

"The Six Kings? The *empress* is in command here. She rules here—and elsewhere!" Darcus Cannu looked at her. It was his last appeal, a last pale chance—but surely his only one. She turned to face him and their eyes met, the slim girlish empress on her great throne and the purple-robed man who had so long advised her father—and slain him.

Valeron noted that Jallad of Nyor still stood beside her, sword sheathed. *Perhaps the boy thinks he's ready to protect her,* Valeron thought. *But—standing there alone, sword at side, whilst we fought? Cool enough of face, nigh imperious—like an emperor watching loyal subjects rid him of the disloyal!*

Jheru and I fought—and Lexton, and Vidul and Eshara, aye and fat Narran ol-Shalkh too—while Aleysha and Jallad watched. And . . . Darcus Cannu, for he took no opportunity to help his hirelings—took no chances himself!

"Valeron of Branarius is my legate," Aleysha ca Velquain said. "I appointed him in person and by letter. With *my* dagger he freed himself of *your* imprisonment. In my name he has returned."

EIGHTEEN
Siense and . . . Science

DARCUS Cannu gasped as realization of this damned girl's shrewdness and treachery—to him—came to him. Those innocent eyes! That passive malleability —lies! The flat voiced statement and her accusing eyes showed it him then; he had erred. *He* had underestimated her by far; *he* had been *wrong*.

She *was* empress.

"You! Oh, Aleysha! It *had* to be done; your father intended that you *wed* that barbarous savage you call legate."

"I am aware of that, Darcus."

"So! So that is the way of it. Oh, by the gods! Empress or no, you still think with the mind of an impressionable child!"

The prime minister turned to the others, raised appealing hands. They stared at him, warriors and warrior-kings and a warrior-woman lately a slave. Their eyes were flat and cold; naked swords hung shiny and red-smeared at the ends of their arms.

"My *lords and lady* Kings! Hear! The emperor grew *old*. He saw a strong warrior conquer and unite a world thought lost; he remembered a time past—long past— when *he* was a strong warrior. Old, the emperor's poor tired mind hit upon a match between his daughter and *this man*." Darcus watched them; saw that their faces had not changed. His tone was earnest, pleading for understanding. "Oh my *lords!* It is true that our beloved Velquen was once a strong warrior . . . but *never* a jungle animal like this hot-eyed atavist I see before me. Lords and lady Kings, I *knew* the emperor. I worked at his side these many years. Such a decision and such an act was not in his nature; this was not the

151

man who was our greatest emperor. This was a man
whose brain was softened by age and the emotion it
substitutes for reason."

"More treason," Vidul said with deadly quietness, the
words slashing like a sword-blade into the prime minister's pause.

"*Not* treason, my lord King. And—"

"Wait, Darcus Cannu," Lexton of Maruthia spoke.
He stepped forward through the groups of armored men
and women. "Wait." Glancing down, he seemed to note
the sword in his hand for the first time, and he sheathed
it. "We have come to arrest you. There will be a trial,
later. Before all of us, as befits your station. You need
not place yourself on trial *now*."

"But I am, my lord King. I have with me no fear of
trial—but fear is with me that *this man*"—he gestured
at Valeron—"I may never live to stand trial."

"Nonsense!" The new voice was Eshara's. "He is
guilty of treason and the worst of murders. Now he attempts to cloud—"

"Pardon asked, my lady King, but—*not* treason,"
Darcus Cannu said.

"You—you dare interrupt one of the *kings*, little
man?" Vidul demanded.

"I dare—I who dared slay an emperor for the good
of Empire—I dare, aye. . . as you, my lord *King*, dared
slay a king for the good of his kingdom!" Darcus Cannu
paused, saw that none would speak for the nonce, and
hurried on. "I apologize to the empress for my words
about her father. They were not kind. Is belief with you
that I liked them? I *loved* Velquen. No, my lords and
ladies, truth be not treason. You have followed *this
man*. Why? Because he is a brilliant tactician. A warrior
without peer. But what else is he? Can you follow him
in *peace*?"

Darcus Cannu returned their stares, his eyes moving
among them. All were hostile. He went on, still pleading
that they might see what he saw, what he had seen.

"Can you picture him on this throne here beside me,
this barbarian? Can you picture your royal selves bending a knee to *this man*?—calling him Eminence, and
Sire, and knowing you are all more civilized, more intel-

ligent than he—and *fearing* him precisely because of
that? Can you conceive of an emperor in the seagreen
robes of Empire—*without sleeves?* An *emperor*, vainly
baring the muscular brawn of a barbarian conqueror?
Can you picture this man—again, Your Eminence, I
plead for your pardon," he interrupted himself, with a
bow to Aleysha.

He was aware of the eyes, aware that their owners
were listening; aware of the frowning glances that the
soldiers and the kings turned upon one another, upon
the bare-armed giant standing among them. He towered
over all save Lexton, and his eyes were feral gleaming
slits. The longsword was ugly and naked in his naked
fist, and as sinister as Vidul's face. Daringly, aware that
he had them arrested, listening and thinking, Darcus
Cannu went on in a lower voice, sibilant and accusing.

"Can you picture that red-handed hulk abed with the
daughter of Velquen?"

Beside him the slim young empress gasped, gasped
and lifted her chin. Her breasts strained and rippled the
cloth of her gown with her agitated breathing. She
stared straight ahead; she was empress.

"Can you imagine the offspring of barbarous Branarius, raised by Sungol raiders, occupying the Imperial
Seat, deciding the fates of your successors, claiming
their fealty?" Darcus Cannu paused, looking from one
to the other to another.

The Branarians glared their hatred at him. The
others . . . looked at Valeron. Perhaps they had seen
him before, perhaps they hadn't. Perhaps they were
seeing him anew, perhaps for the first time. Eshara
glanced about, met Lexton's eyes. They frowned.

"I avow innocence of treason," the prime minister
said, in a voice steadily low and quiet. "I acted to *protect* the throne, to protect Empire. I will not see it given
into the hands of a bloody barbarian conqueror without
his having even to conquer it! The emperor was *old,* too
old. He would have handed over Aleysha to this man.
She is a young girl, and would be easily dominated by
such a man. I loved Velquen! I love Aleysha, and I love
the Empire of the Six Worlds too much to see this hap-
pen. I tried to talk with Velquen—to no avail. At last I

decided that I must try, as I always have, to save Empire, no matter what the measures necessary—or the consequences."

"Murder," Vidul muttered, drawing the word out.

"My lord King Valeron," Lexton said, "I ask that your Prefect Burgon and these others leave this hall. The prime minister is determined to stand trial here and now, and I am ready to accommodate him!"

Valeron only turned and nodded. The soldiers left.

From his place beside Aleysha, Jallad of Nyor descended the steps and walked out to where the kings stood. He turned. The Six Kings faced Darcus Cannu.

"The Council of Kings," Eshara said, "is met."

"Do you deny murdering the emperor?" Lexton asked.

He and the other kings stood a couple of meters removed from the foot of the dais; a strange trial it was, in which the accused stood in the place of honor beside the high seat and looked down on his accusers and judges.

"Murder? Aye, I deny murdering him."

Vidul snorted and slapped his thigh with a black-gauntleted hand. "Ahhhh! Do you deny *assassinating*, then? Do you deny doing death on the emperor?"

"I gave the order that he die, yes," Darcus Cannu said, and at the plain words at last there was from all of them the sound of sharply indrawn breaths.

"Do you deny," Lexton asked, in a lower voice, "deliberately accusing this innocent man and planning his death to save yourself?"

"I do deny it. I did accuse him—but to save Empire, not myself."

Lexton sighed and laid a hand on Vidul's arm when the black-armored Laviani started to speak in exasperation. "You make no denial of falsely accusing, attacking, imprisoning, and planning the death of the lord Valeron, Warlord of Branarius, for a crime he did not commit?"

"I do not."

"Do you deny, Darcus car Nu called Cannu, arranging an obscenely hurried marriage to Aleysha in order that you might seize control of the Imperial Seat?"

"*Obscene? Seize* control?"

"Prime Minister!" Lexton called. "You do violence on our patience! You accomplish nothing here by this playing with words—it reeks of mockery of the Council of Kings. Did you not arrange a hasty marriage with Her Eminence; did you not plan to rule through her?"

"Aye. Because I believe the years have proven my ability, and I felt that I could better serve Empire that way. Youth is no longer with me. By the time of my death, I reasoned—*reasoned*, my lords and lady Kings—Her Eminence would have matured to an ability to administer and rule. She is intelligent and highborn and already, I do assurance on you, she is mature beyond her years." He glanced at her. "And more capable of dissemblance than I had supposed!"

"An interesting point," Narran ol-Shalkh said. "I am convinced, my lords and lady Kings, that he acted on behalf of Empire, not from personal ambition."

"Aye," Eshara said slowly. "Aye ... I believe the man. Belief is with me that he speaks the truth; he did what he did for the reasons he has stated."

"And I say he is a contemptible damned murdering liar," Vidul said, with vicious vehemence.

Eshara shook her head. "I know Darcus Cannu ... and I believe ... that he thought first of Empire, as ... as he has for years."

"Your Eminence and Kings."

They looked at the speaker: Jallad of Nyor. The youngest—and seemingly most frail, in his youthful slimness—of the group, and aware of it, he had but listened until now. "Fear is with me that whether Darcus Cannu speaks true or no is aside from the point. We discuss treason and murder."

Eyes widened and foreheads creased. Valeron and the others gazed at him, waiting. Jallad glanced around at them. His voice, which was not deep, he held carefully low.

"Much talk have we heard," Jallad said, "of 'barbarous' and 'barbarian' and 'red-handed savage' and such like. They were applied to King Valeron, whom we are not here to judge. Already he has been judged, and his presence here is evidence of your decision. My presence among you is evidence of my concurrence. For nigh onto two weeks I have abode here in the palace; I have talked with the Empress and heard her speak. Now have we heard Darcus Cannu speak in justification of his acts. There was—and is—justification in his own mind, and I have heard the lady King Eshara agree. Yet . . . what *were* those actions of Darcus Cannu, the trusted minister, the chief counselor and confidant of the emperor? He would have us forget those naked acts of themselves. Forget not that he is on trial—with his head in the hangman's *noose*."

The youngest king raised his left hand, folding down its fingers with his right, one by one.

"Plotting against the throne—regardless of motive: the *throne* of Empire. Bribery of the Palatine Guard—regardless of motive: the guardians of Empire." With his eyes on Darcus he slowly folded down the third finger and spoke the next word slowly, in two long syllables. "Murder. Regardless of motive, the murder of the emperor himself—*the barbarous act of a red-handed savage*. Was Velquen evil, that he must be murdered to save Empire?" Another finger folded. "Falsely accusing and immuring King Valeron. Regardless of motive—a crime, each of those acts. But each of them combines to form a higher crime, one that challenges law and Empire and this Council of Kings. Into his own hands Darcus Cannu has taken the right to judge and execute, the very law itself—without consultation with any of us. In advance, he decided that his wisdom and his judgment were superior to ours. . . to the law."

Jallad's grimly held face relaxed into a smile and he shrugged.

"It may be true," he said. "But—this man now attempts to mask his *barbaric* behavior as solemn heroic statesmanship. Here we stand, my lords and lady kings, and who among us is the barbarian? This man?" Jallad moved past Lexton to touch Valeron's arm, then paced on, away from the silent big man. "Or . . . *this?*"

The Nyori king's arm swung toward Darcus Cannu, finger outstretched.

And there was silence.

"*By the gods!*" Narran whispered. "He is *right!*"

Eshara spoke thoughtfully. "Barbarism expresses itself in *acts*. No matter what the motives, Darcus Cannu, you are guilty. It's you have acted barbarically. Altruism is no excuse for barbarism."

"Of course he is guilty," Vidul rumbled, and Lexton nodded.

Lexton said, "It has taken Valeron of Branarius to lead us into a *civilized* campaign, an entry here with the absolute minimum possible of bloodshed. The so-called barbarian among us has shown us civilized ways. And the youngest among us has shown us wisdom; the true meaning of barbarism. Eshara of Sid-Alors has shown us that altruism can be a crime. And . . . I call all to note as I have that my lord King Valeron has spoken no word during this trial. We are agreed, Darcus Cannu."

Lexton turned to the others, stepping away a little so that he faced them all; the Council of Kings. "The sentence?"

Wiped and sheathed, Vidul's blade scraped out anew. Eshara's eyes, sad but certain, were on the prime minister as she lifted her sword in the signal of guilt. Narran's curved Ghulani blade swished from its oiled scabbard. Slowly, Jallad drew. And Lexton.

The condemning swords lifted like silver fangs to flash and gleam in the soft glow of the Ancient-lights.

Lexton turned to Valeron. "And the Sixth King?"

Valeron drew steel slowly. "You have passed judgment, and named the sentence," he said. "It was not for me to judge. Now I concur." He took a step nearer the dais, his eyes fixed on the face of Darcus Cannu.

"Your Eminence," Lexton said, "the Council of Kings finds Darcus Cannu guilty of all charges; motive notwithstanding, no individual may do what he has done. By unanimous agreement, the sentence is death."

Darcus Cannu spread wide his purple-gowned arms. "See, see! The future emperor! The future father of the empress's children! The arbiter of justice, the administrator of Empire, the liege-lord of all. See how he advances upon me with drawn glaive twice blooded in this hall! He raises the bloody steel of barbarism to stop this brain and heart which sought to serve and protect.

I cannot compete with a sword and brawn . . . *I have but intelligence to offer.*"

Valeron smiled. "You lose once again, Prime Minister. I come to take you in custody on behalf of the Council of Kings, not to do death on you. We others here are *civilized* men and women."

Deliberately Valeron halted at the foot of the dais and sheathed his sword. . . and Darcus Cannu's hand suddenly contained a slender rod of black metal. Valeron stared at that dozen centimeters of hollow metal, while Darcus Cannu spoke.

"My lords and lady Kings! I have acted only for the welfare of Empire! I sought to save it from a senile emperor . . . an impressionable girl . . . and a red-handed savage! He, in his primitive ignorance, found the machinery of the Ancients. He found this weapon—and ignored it! I refuse arrest, and I reject your judgment. But I accept your sentence—for King Jallad is right! I had thought myself the only civilized man present—I find I was wrong. He is: Jallad of Nyor. Ponder the good fortune of us all, of Empire, that he is unwed and the empress's age! Aye, I was dragged down; you see how barbarism and fear of it drags us down! After a lifetime as a man of intellect without violence, I was *forced* to violence by fear of this man Valeron. And now he forces me to violence again. Aye, I accept your sentence . . . and my last act will be to execute that sentence on myself. But first—I save you from him!"

He raised the black cylinder of the Ancients before that river of wide-staring eyes. "This tube will drill a fiery hole more terrible than the unwieldy weapon of barbarism you brandish, *my lord barbarian!* I, in the name of Siense, pronounce judgment on this man: death by Siense, the only way we can save ourselves from barbarism!"

The prime minister stretched a loose-sleeved arm to level the rod at Valeron's chest.

There was a crackling, a hornet-like humming; a bluish light glimmered and danced. A strange odor heavied the air as flame licked out—and Darcus Cannu stiffened, seemed to whiten, to glow and shimmer in the very air.

Then he vanished.

Bedlam! A clamor of voices babbled excited exclamations and questions. Bedlam!—broken by a rather high-pitched call that lowered itself quickly to the carefully controlled tones of a young man aware of the weakness of his voice.

"Aye," Jallad of Nyor said, when the others quieted. "Death by Siense is the sentence; and it *is* our savior." He raised his hand to show them a dull black rod similar to the one that had disappeared with Darcus Cannu. "His Ancient-weapon, he said, would have drilled a fiery hole. The bolt of lightening-energy loosed by this one we found on Nyor in our excavating researches— and which we *understand*, my lords and ladies—this one disintegrates whatever it touches. Completely and finally."

His face was not triumphant as the young monarch pushed the cylinder with its disguising dagger hilt back into the strange round sheath on his right hip.

The others stared at the willowy young genius of Nyor.

Eshara sundered the long silence. "One ... one of you has saved Empire," she said.

At the sound of her words the stasis of shock ended and movement returned to the great hall. It began with the empress. Sinking back into the Imperial Seat she tried desperately to hold herself rigidly in it by sheer force of will and physical strength. Her thin hands thrust up their knuckles as she clutched the chair arms—as she clutched consciousness. But she failed; she swayed, her grip relaxed, her eyes fluttered, and Aleysha collapsed.

"Leysha!" As that mass of foam-colored hair swung forward, Jallad bounded past Valeron to catch her. He swung the young woman up into his arms.

They stepped aside, the other kings, silent and stony as the marble female figures that lined the Hall of a Hundred Women. Jallad paced wordlessly down the crimson carpet among kings and corpses, and out through the great doors, with the empress limp in his arms.

As he exited, the doors swung wide and soldiers streamed into the throne room once more.

Amid the noise, Narran ol-Shalkh spoke thoughtfully to Eshara; thoughtfully, and quietly indeed. "One of them saved the empire, aye. Jallad . . . or Valeron . . . or Darcus Cannu. But . . . *which one?*"

NINETEEN
Edgeman and Edgewoman

RANKHNAX of Sungol ran into the vast hall less than a minute after Jallad had left with Aleysha. Behind him hurried warriors of Maruthia.

"My brother! Alerku and his Carmeians have gone into a passage in the wall of the council chamber. They have locked it from the other side."

Valeron's eyes lashed at him. *"Where does it lead?"*

Rankhnax shook his head. They heard the furor in the corridor now; loud voices, running feet, shouted questions that outnumbered replies and shouted instructions.

"Get you to the gate," Vidul ordered one of his men. "Warn them and post men from the shipfield to all city gates—but *outside*. Do *not* raise a fuss in the city. Sense—the city!" He turned to stare at the others.

"I'll go out," Lexton said, and Maruthia's king hurried from the throne-room to the big front doors of the palace.

"Follow and guard him," Valeron snapped, to the Maruthians. "With your lives."

The men of Maruthia rushed after their king.

"Aleysha . . ." Eshara muttered, and her robe swirled about her mailed legs as she too hurried from the Hall of a Hundred Women.

The coup had been brilliant in plan and execution, smooth and relatively simple. The people of the capital of Empire were not even aware of the "invasion" and the toppling of Darcus Cannu, just as they had not been aware of his perfidy. But now Valeron knew that a few of Alerku's men could spread the word rapidly—on and in their own terms. They had to be found and stopped. Else chaos could well erupt; innocent Carmeians as well

as soldiers from all the worlds would die in a bloody
civil strife because of lies and misunderstandings.

Ignoring the others, Vidul turned to Valeron. "A
door from the council room . . . a door Alerku knew
of . . ."

Valeron nodded and his eyes widened in revelation.
"Darcus!" he said, and began to move. "Cannu's
office—it probably leads there, through the palace
walls!"

The two edgemen-kings ran.

By the time they reached Darcus Cannu's office on
the palace's second floor, Valeron's Branarians and
Vidul's Laviani were at their backs. Into that purple
room they burst, swords shining naked in their fists.
Across the room a magenta drapery flapped awry. Behind it a narrow door hung open, and Valeron plunged
through. He peered down a narrow dark stair. He
paused to listen, but heard no sound from below. Via
this secret stair Alerku had ascended here. And . . .

"They came this way," he said, returning to Vidul
and the knot of edgemen standing on Darcus Cannu's
purple carpet.

"But—" One of Valeron's men stared at him, frowning. "Warlord: none has left this room!"

"I'm glad sureness is with you, Barderon. Then we
can be sure of how they *did* leave." He took long strides
and a stab of his finger soon exposed to them the in-
terior of the room-that-moved. "This will take us to a
cavern beneath the palace dungeons."

Vidul stared into the little room of the Ancients.
"This madhouse of a palace is a honeycomb of hidden
doorways and passages. Kroy himself must have been
designer . . . This will *take us down?* I see but a tiny
room with one door."

Valeron explained quickly—within his limited
ability—about the room-that-rose-and-lowered, trying
to give them some idea of what to expect when the door
opened below.

"Now, Vidul. You must wait briefly. Count to . . . oh,
ten tens. Then push this button. You will feel it when
you have reached bottom and the room has come to a
stop. Then push *this* button, and be ready—they may

be waiting for you. There is another way down. I'll take it. We cannot run the risk of walking into a trap. How many were there, Rankhnax?"

"Alerku and a half-score, Sanxarkhl my brother." The golden-eyed Sungol touched Valeron's arm. "My brother is now chief of all Branarius, and this man is king, too, on his world. It were better neither of you went below. We edgemen will deal with these treacherous Carmeians, Sanxarkhl."

Vidul looked at Rankhnax with a warrior's regard for another good soldier—and good subject; the same race-transcending bond of regard that led Valeron and the hairless, golden-eyed Sungol to call each other "brother."

"I go," Vidul said quietly, and his tone and manner left no room for argument.

"We all go," Valeron said. "Barderon ... Mohammon ... Stanel ... Gregon: come along." He looked at Vidul. "To ten tens."

"It will strain both my patience and my mind," Vidul said, and his dark smile was as humorless and thin as the Branarian's.

Valeron stopped to bid Burgon continue the close watch: "For all knowledge with me, there may be still another way into this place from the caverns," he said. "Guard the kings. That fat Narran certainly cannot defend himself. And—watch Jheru, Burgon."

Valeron, Rankhnax, and the other four Branarians yanked open the door to the dungeon and boiled down the steps. They reached first floor level in night-darkness; turned and patted the wall, found more steps. Down they went, and stone-faced wood gave onto the dungeon. A solitary guard, staring, willingly backed into a cell. He knew nothing of what had taken place above, nor did Valeron take time to explain that this was not an invasion from the Barbarian World. The Carmeian, eyes on the Sungol, was locked in the cubicle.

The six Branarians trotted down the dungeon corridor, pulling torches from cressets bolted into the walls. When they arrived at the cell of the well-remembered trapdoor, Valeron turned to his little force.

"My hope is to come upon Alerku and his men from two directions at once," he said, for he had long given his followers at least some idea of his plans; they became thus part of the enterprise, rather than cattle-driven soldiers. "I know but two ways to reach him: the moving room we left to the Laviani—and this less pleasant way. This—is a trapdoor. We must drop through, one at a time. We will fall, then slide, and we will fetch up at bottom in darkness. Hold high your torches and *don't let go*." He had indicated the concealed door in the floor, with his toe.

"Allow me, brother," Rankhnax said, and he shouldered his king aside to step on the counterbalanced stone. It tripped; the Sungol shot down and the block was back in place before Valeron could prevent him.

He waited a moment, then followed.

Again Valeron car Nadh fell into darkness. Again his body struck a smooth chute, and again he swept down into murk—this time lit flickeringly by Rankhnax's glim. The Sungol scrambled aside; his commander slid down at his feet with a grunt. Valeron rose. The two from Branarius looked at each other a moment. The hairless man's thin lips smiled.

"How the children of Branarius would love this chute, brother! I see naught ahead save blackness. The Carmeians must be farther on. We— Have care!"

Valern stepped back to make way as another man whooshed down, managing to hold his torch high. Another followed. Then another, and finally Barderon came sliding down to sprawl with grunts and a curse. A torch had been dropped and had gone out; it was quickly relit.

"Now we shall—"

Valeron broke off and reached for his sword when the stone in the cell above scraped, clunked, banged back into place.

"*Uh!*" Another warrior came sliding down, flailing; a warrior in the serpent-crested sallet and baggy trousers of Ghulan. Valeron bent forward to examine this follower—and groaned. He cursed. She was barely recognizable in the chaincoat and the face-covering helmet with its narrow vision slit.

"Jheru! You incredible foolish woman! Why did you follow us?"

She got wincing to her feet and clapped her hand, with a grimace, to her backside. "I go where you go, incredible foolish king. Those were Her Eminence's instructions to me her dutiful slave, remember?" Jheru smiled.

"Kroy take you—you will remain here! We have edgemen's work to do. And when we return it will be *my* hand you'll feel on your backside—and it will not be soothing! Damn!" He turned to the grinning quintet of Branarians. "Wipe those stupid smiles from your stupid faces and come."

"Hmp!" Jheru commented. "My lord *barbarian!*"

Valeron led his men forward into the darkness of the cavern, with Rankhnax crowding him, trying to protect the conqueror king by pushing past to be first—while Jheru followed. They halted, glancing about with fearful eyes as after two more steps the tunnel was flooded with the soft light of men dead and gone in the mists of pasts. Jheru and the Branarians gawked and muttered at the immense body of the mechanical serpent; looked with renewed respect on their leader when he advised quietly that he had done death on it. Jheru remembered the wound he'd borne when he emerged from this place, seemingly months and months ago.

Valeron smiled upon them with a father's condescending expression, enjoying himself, looking as if he wondered how edgemen of Branarius could be such children as to be frightened by mere Ancient-magic—as he had been but two weeks before.

Then he realized that Jheru had not remained behind. He took an angry step toward her—

He was brought to a halt by the sound of clashing steel and the loud cries of men. He spun about and lunged along the tunnel without waiting to see if his men followed. They did, running along the subterrene corridor, rounding a vermiform double turn, and coming upon the source of the combative noise.

With the Laviani trapped in the room-that-moved and hampering each other's attempts to fight free, Alerku's men had the obvious better of the clangorous encounter. The little room-that-moved afforded no space for maneuvering or swinging a curved Lavi blade. Two of the men of Lavian were down, and but one Carmeian had a wound on him. As Valeron's little band caught sight of them, another Laviani edgeman groaned and fell forward beneath the feet of the attackers. And Vidul's right cheek bled from the shallow slice of a Carmeian blade.

"YAH BRANARIII!" Rankhnax bellowed, and he charged past Valeron to plunge his sword deep into the back of the rearmost Carmeian. The Sungol had shouted his loud cry; it was not his fault if the stupid enemy moved more slowly than he and had not turned to meet the charge.

Men whirled at the shout, and some turned to meet the new attack—too many. Without a trace of emotion on his cold face Vidul lunged from the little room to drive his curving sword into the throat of a Palatine Guardsman. His remaining men burst forth from their trap.

Then in the ancient cavern beneath the Imperial Palace began the final struggle in the plot against the throne—and for the throne.

A half-score Carmeians, chosen as imperial bodyguards on the basis of their swordsmanship, faced men whose abilities had brought them through the wars of two planets. Gaudily attired Carmeians were attacked by a shrieking daemon with yellow eyes and no bodily hair, by six bull-roaring barbarians; by the dark sinister man from Lavian with his icy eyes and four followers—and by a very young woman in the helmet, armor, and loose breeches of a Ghulani edgeman.

Swords clanged and shrieked off blade and armor as Ancient-made steel met Ancient steel. Cries of war and of pain and the horror of bloody dying echoed and re-echoed along the subterranean corridor of seeming sorcery. The scarlet flow and smear of blood mingled with the viscous gray of brainstuff and the pink of erupting entrails and broadswords and scimitars thrust and pierced and chopped and clove.

One of Valeron's picked men staggered back, both hands clutching his belly. Mohammon car Jairron, slayer of a score of Sungoli and survivor of the Branarian Battle of Highpeak, staggered back against an Ancient-made wall with liquid crimson seeping between his fingers. He slid slowly down to the floor. Before his slayer had time to rejoice, Valeron's meter-long sword chopped down into his shoulder. The blade went deep, the Palatine twisted as he fell groaning, and Valeron's long glaive was dragged from his grasp.

Booting a side attacker in the leg so hard he was spun half about, Valeron lunged after the sword. As he laid hold of the pommel he glanced up to see another Carmeian take a long step across the body of the fallen Branarian. As if in Kroy-sent hypnosis, Valeron saw the man swing high his gleaming blade of death. Valeron yanked at Jimarah's black hilt, twisted and felt it slide free—and his foot slipped on the gore-splashed floor.

He fell heavily, trying to twist away from the downcoming blade of the Carmeian.

The sword dropped clanging from dead fingers. The man stiffened and his knees buckled. A broad blade stood quivering in his groin. He took one disjointed step backward, staring at the protruding hilt, and crashed back and down. Before he was supine, edgeman's reflexes spurred Valeron to his feet with the sinuous speed of a mountain cat. He glanced with an ugly smile at his savior—and his expression became an astonished stare.

Jheru flashed him a brief smile and bowed, briefly, before stepping swiftly past him to retrieve her spearhurled sword.

The Warlord of Branarius cursed in two languages. Saved by a woman! The ignominy of it! How dared the wench! He—he'd ... thank her, later, and show her that winners were sometimes raped, too.

But not now—and mayhap they'd not be winners at all.

Now swords flashed and clashed with frightful steely clangs and grating whines all about him, ringing on aching eardrums in that underground chamber. The cries of men met and rent in the air with the discordant din of their arms; Alerku and his band fought with savage desperation. All knew there could be no pardon for them if they surrendered. This battle, each individual fight, must be to the death, and men with such knowledge became far more dangerous than normally. With that understanding, their opponents, too, battled the harder. The iron clamor was deafening. The Laviani and Branarii had good reason to wish fervently that their leaders had brought more men. Even odds were hardly even, when the foe had become cornered animals made savage and carelessly valiant by their very desperation.

Steel rang and screeched on bluish Ancient steel as clutching fingers chopped and lunged and slashed and parried and slashed yet again. The offworlders had entered the palace armored and armed; Valeron had not dared allow them to carry bucklers, lest they arouse alarm to result in alarums. And the Palatine Guard never carried bucklers—and practiced at sword-against-sword defense.

"My man, lord King," Vidul shouted, and Valeron realized that the man whose blade he'd just beat away from his midsection was Alerku.

Valeron shook his head violently. "My man, lord King!" he growled low in his throat.

He swept aside Alerku's next lunge with a backhand sweep of his sword. Though that blade was both heavy and overlong, Valeron's arms were the size of many men's legs. He did not swing his sword back into defensive line, but wrenched it back at Alerku's face.

The Carmeian Prefect of Palatines avoided death by a fraction of a centimeter. Still he fell back a pace with a trickling lines of red across his chin. He feinted and whipped his own point up to guard.

"My lord *barbarian,* I believe," he said between tight lips, and his reddened sword leaped forward in a long lunge.

Valeron felt the point touch the leather of his Carmeian cuirass as he strove to suck in his chest and hurl himself backward. His fast-sweeping sword halted Alerku's follow-up with a terrible clanging clash of blades. Alerku avoided the leaping tip of Valeron's point; already the Carmeian had learned respect for the offworlder's ability to handle that great glaive as though it were but a stick.

As Valeron tensed for a forward spring, steel sang to his left and a trousered warrior stumbled back from a vicious attack.

Directly into Alerku, Jheru staggered, and his left arm shot out to cross her body in front and clutch her right wrist. He enfolded her against himself. This Valeron saw only from the tail of his eye, for he glanced at Jheru's attacker to see the man stepping past him, sword leveled to split the mailed woman while Alerku held her.

Valeron half-wheeled. His sword flashed around in a viciously powerful forehand swing of rage that drove its edge through bronze-bossed leather corselet and skin and soft flesh beyond. The guardsman fell with blood gouting forth from his stomach, his body held together by his backbone and a thin strand of flesh—and his cuirass.

"*Hold*, my lord *barbarian!*" Alerku shouted. "Hold or I slice this bitch open like a ripe melon—an *over*-ripe melon!"

Jheru writhed in the prefect's grasp, but Alerku was no weakling and she was unable to twist free. Valeron stared, watching the man's eyes, watching them flit about to shoot glances this way and that. Alerku's brows came down and his face paled.

"So." His voice, too, had gone pale. "I am the last. I have the choice—fight on, or surrender, or flee. Stay back!" He jerked at Jheru and let his sword's edge touch her throat. His eyes swept over the half-crouched men who faced him with naked, crimson-smeared swords. "Suicide I like not, and fighting against so many would be foolish. Could be only one sentence pronounced on me, too, if I surrender. No! Stay away, all of you damned offworlders! I am forced to leave you. Stand away from the moving room; this *slavegirl* and I are departing your company."

Alerku's gaze fixed on Valeron's; the two men stared.

"I followed the wrong man," the prefect said.

Valeron nodded, his eyes measuring, his brain weighing the chances of Jheru's death when he charged, as he must . . .

"Well ... too late to join you now, King Valeron.
Come—on, wench!"

Valeron tensed to leap—and heard the little wind-
sigh. He felt the gentlest of breezes as a dagger flashed
past his cheek from behind. It passed Jheru's helmeted
head, too—to bury itself to a carven Sungoli hilt in
Alerku's throat.

Still holding Jheru, the Palatine Prefect staggered
back against the wall. His uplifted right arm was trembling, straining to open Jheru's throat even as he died.

Valeron of Branarius lunged in a long passado. His
sword-point pierced Prefect Alerku's sword-arm. The
Carmeian's weapon dropped from blood-slippery fingers. His hand tightened on Jheru's wrist and with the
wounded arm he sought to clutch her face. But the
motions were spasmodic; his hands lurched twitching
from her as he shuddered and slid down the wall with
the dagger still standing from his neck.

Jheru sprang away from him, but stopped just short
of Valeron. She gazed at him, and the pain in her eyes
was partially reflected in his; the pain was not physical.

"Even," Valeron said. "I repay my debt to you
quickly, edgewoman. No wish is with me to owe you my
life."

She stared, a pace from him. Her half-raised arms
dropped to her sides. "I do not make apology for saving
it," the empress's former slavegirl said very quietly.
" 'When death is with you ... I, too, die.' "

Silence lay on them all, save for the groaning of
wounded men; the others stared at the ruler of Branarius and the slave-turned-edgewoman who loved him and
had just said so, in the words of his own people.

Then she lifted her head and said, "Besides, I think
yon Sungol repaid your debt for you."

With a scowl, Valeron turned to Rankhnax, who was
wearing his evil Sungoli smile.

"My brother knows I took no chances," he said. "No
man throws a dagger with the speed or skill of a Sungol."

Valeron inclined his head. "You took no chance. It
was well done," he said, and made the Sungoli gesture.

"And what if you had missed," Vidul asked, half-grinning, with blood crusted on his cheek and chin. "What if he had moved just as you threw—and you had sunk that dagger in her"—he glanced at Jheru, gauging—"mouth?"

"Then he would not have had a hostage," Rankhnax said, with a little shrug, nor did he seem to note Jheru's stare.

Alerku and his men lay dead, strewn about the cavern floor amid the bodies of slain and sorely wounded Branarians and Laviani. Rankhnax dropped to a wounded man of his planet; other men saw to other slashed or spitted allies. Across the jumbled tangle of corpses, Vidul gazed, to meet Valeron's eyes. He glanced down, transferred his blooded and nicked sword to his left hand, and stepped forward.

The two men gripped wrists.

"You and yours are noble allies worth fighting alongside, Valeron of Branarius."

"And you and the men of Lavian, Vidul. With you by me I had won Branarius a year and more sooner."

"Alliance is with Lavian and Branarius, Valeron, so long as I live. In Lav's name, I swear."

Valeron nodded. "You supported me in the throne room, King Vidul, above all others. It might have been more to your advantage to remain silent while Darcus car Nu did condemnation on me."

"Aye. He confirmed that you are Velquen's chosen, King Valeron, and evidently the empress's, as well as her legate. I support Empire; I am king of a Lavian I rescued from a tyrant, not a conqueror who'd do challenge on the highest throne."

Valeron gazed into the darkly bearded man's eyes, which with nose and lower lip were all of Vidul's features bare of curling black hair. "You claim fealty to him who sits the highest throne?"

"Unless that person attacks or challenges my world, I *owe* fealty, Valeron of Branarius, to the highest throne itself, and the crown—and whoever sits on that throne and wears that crown of Empire."

"Vidul . . . you would do well to make that statement aloud, in the presence of the other kings."

Vidul's eyes went cold and flat. "Let them worry and wonder," he said, and almost he smiled.

Beside Valeron, Rankhnax laughed—not a pretty sound from those vocal cords and through those teeth. He inclined his hairless head. "The Sungoli are allied with the Hairmen because of Sanxarkhl whom you call Valeron, Hairman King of Lavian. The Sungoli call no Hairman brother, save Sanxarkhl whom you call Valeron. And now you."

"Rankhnax—" Vidul began.

"Lovely, my lords," a voice interrupted. "Meanwhile we stand knee-deep in blood and gore and more than one of your bleeding men stands through sheer strength of will. Can we not go elsewhere for the trading of these manly speeches of good will and eternal love?"

The men turned to face the pantalooned warrior-woman with the mass of black hair escaping her helmet and the extraordinary swell of her shining Ghulani chest-armor. At their stares, Jheru placed hands on hips and threw apart her legs.

"I kiss my sword to you, warrioress," Rankhnax said.

Valeron ignored the Sungol's formal declaration of respect and the word he had bastardly created from the Sungoliye for "wielder of deadly weapons," which was masculine only.

"Now by Branar and Siense, *blowze*," Valeron told the staring woman, "*now* is the time you receive that rump-slapping we have discussed before!"

"You will pardon the offer of help from an ally, Valeron," Vidul said, his grin aimed hungrily at Jheru, "but I think it may take both of us to hold her."

Taking a long forward step, Rankhnax wheeled, and was at Jheru's side. He slid an arm across her back and onto her shoulder. "What would you of my sister the warrior Jheru—*Hairmen?*"

The kings stared, exchanged a look, and shook their heads.

"Hmp," Jheru snorted. "*I* know . . . *brother* Rankhnax. One at least wants me in my present stance, but without armor—and not vertical."

Even wounded men laughed.

TWENTY

Empress and Kings . . . and Barbarian

VALERON and Vidul had just entered the Hall of a Hundred Women when Aleysha, too, returned. She entered the presence of the kings apologetically, leaning on the arm of the young monarch of Nyor. Jallad was most attentive, and she was smiling at some remark he had just made.

At his belt he wore the strange cylindrical sheath containing that which boded so much change for them all, for the people of the Seven Worlds of the Empire of Carmeis, for good or for bad.

Aleysha was empress; knees bent to her, even Eshara's stiff, mailed shanks.

Valeron rose slowly from his genuflection of fealty, his eyes on the slim young man beside the empress. *He has been here every day for two weeks. They have become well acquainted. And when she was fainting, it was Jallad who leaped with concern and attentiveness to catch—and the cry that jerked from him was her name. More, it was not "Eminence" or "Empress" or even "Aleysha"—he cried "Leysha."*

And Valeron heard King Eshara murmur to King Narran, "What a pretty young couple those two make!"

When he shifted his gaze to Aleysha's face, Valeron found her eyes on him. One small hand started to rise, started toward him, then stiffened at her side. "My lords and lady Kings," she began, and the Empress Aleysha accepted their fealty.

At the scintillating dinner that night Valeron was careful to sit well down the long table from the vision at its head. On Aleysha's left was Saldon, the oldest man present; at his left sat Jallad, the youngest. He was an-

173

swering the Elder's questions: Aye, his Elders—young Elders—had repaired a defective airlock on his flagship just last month; yes, they really did understand the principle of the awful weapon he had unleashed in the throne-room. But—did Saldon know that the ways of healing wounds were many, and that some of the old ways were patently wrong, and too, there was a new theory about thoroughly washed hands for physicians and midwives? . . .

The young king talked excitedly, though Valeron felt that Jallad was hard put to remain polite with Saldon while devoting his attention and his handsome smile to the empress.

Besides Jallad sat Lexton; on the white-maned Maruthian's left was Jheru.

She had not wanted to attend the triumphant—and rather tense—celebration of the monarchs and their empress. The gallant King of Maruthia had overcome her objections, offered her his arm and thus entered the banquet hall, and seated her between Valeron and himself. She was glorious in yellow velvet set off by his scarlet-cuffed heliotrope robe. Her gown's scooped neck bared the coppery half-bowls of her bosom. The white satin band beneath raised them so that the skin shone and the flesh rippled gelatinously with her every movement. On one side her blue-black hair was drawn back; a single earring of jet-hued plast dangled there, a gift from Vidul.

She was quiet. Regally garbed she was, but slave she was too, despite the golden armlet—a gift from Lexton—that now covered the slave-mark on each arm. Surrounded by glittering monarchy, she was aware of her lack of status here. And she was aware of the giant of a man beside her, at the table's last place but one— and that he seemed gazing more often at the woman at the table's head.

Despite the gala atmosphere, tension hovered over that laden table like a brooding winter-cloud.

All knew that the Hall of a Hundred Women was still being scrubbed of its terra-cotta stains. Strange accents and strange uniforms colored the air of the capital. Armed guards from the Seven Worlds patrolled the streets and the very halls of the palace. There were decisions to be made, trials to be held, executions to carry out, appointments to be made. A prime minister, a new Palatine Guard and commander . . . new defenses at the shipfield . . . new pacts among the worlds and some sort of constant communication, a daily shuttling of ships, perhaps . . . these were among many and many tasks that lay ahead.

From its odd rounded sheath on his slim hip protruded the dagger-hilt Jallad car Ahmir had mounted on the end of his terrible Ancient-weapon. It put a new era upon them, that must be coped with.

There was tension, too, that involved the big man who had led the almost bloodless and swiftly successful toppling of Darcus Cannu and his traitorous Palatine Prefect. Minds brooded on Valeron—and on the empress. All the kings had seen dead Velquen's letter to Valeron. All knew and conjectured on its meaning and its implications, which could be of the farthest reaching. The kings remembered too, the *words* of the prime minister. They watched the man from the Barbarian World, and the slim girlish woman at the table's head . . . and King Jallad of Nyor.

None could fail to note that the brilliant young king represented progress, and the future—and that he seldom took his eyes off Aleysha, even while he talked with Saldon of Branarius.

Who was leader of the kings, now? The traditional senior, Lexton, with his swift, agile mind and calming influence? The strongest sword and war-leader, Valeron? The dark man they still half-feared, Vidul—obviously somehow now a fast friend of the Branarian Warlord's? Or the open young man who *knew* Siense, as if they were friends, and possessed his Knowledge?

Had swords suddenly become useless, distances and boundaries and defenses meaningless?

They wondered, and tension rode the wine goblets.

Once Jallad leaned around Lexton—and Jheru, with an easy engaging smile for her—to whisper confidentially to Valeron. "Blessed are you of the gods, son of Nadh! The brilliant strategist's brain of yours. . . that fantastic sword-arm . . . and now must I try to catch the

glance of the empress whilst she looks at you. I warn
you, King Valeron . . . I—I think love for her must
already be with me!"

"And what if she were not empress?" Valeron muttered back, forcing a grin and trying not to see Jheru's
face from the edge of his eyes.

Jallad shrugged and flashed his deceivingly ingenuous
smile. "I'd still be prisoner to her beauty and grace . . .
were she no more than a slave!"

Jallad had no notion of his gaffe. Nothing had been
said of Jheru's status. Both she and Valeron knew what
the others inferred as to their relationship, and neither
cared; only on Ghulan might there be any disap-
proval—indeed, less than respect—for the mistress of a
king. Now Valeron glanced at Jheru's face and saw
stricken eyes and rising color. He bent over his plate
with a small smile—but somehow the hand of the barbarian warlord left the table to slip onto her thigh, and
squeeze lightly.

Meanwhile, Lexton's hand found Jheru's under the
table, and squeezed. Thus doubly did the slave and warrior-woman receive comfort and support—and it was
Valeron's gesture that surprised her, not that of the
most gallant of kings.

"On my world," Lexton murmured, "You are free, as
I have said. And you might be even more . . . if you like
your men old, and crowned." His eyes twinkled, but
Valeron felt that the man was not merely jesting.

Jheru regarded Lexton, and she dared not blink lest
tears suddenly glitter on her cheeks.

Anger rose up in Valeron, anger at Jallad. With his
teeth set in his lip, he forced it down, forced his brain to
work, and he chose his words.

"Almost I am deceived by your boyish smile and
seeming ingenuousness, my lord King of Nyor," he
said, and smiled pleasantly into Jallad's surprised face.

Jallad heaved a sigh. "We men do what we must," he
said, "and what we can, my lord King of Branarius."
And smiling he straightened and addressed himself to
his food.

"I must—there's something I have forgot," Jheru

said, stammering and weak-voiced, and she rose and hurriedly departed the banquet chamber.

"Covering tears," Lexton said to Valeron, very quietly indeed. "She's best alone, for a time."

Valeron nodded—and brooded.

Carefully he had avoided Aleysha's eyes, knowing they sought him often. He thought furiously, desperately, of her softness, of her proud bearing, of that mighty chair of precious plast in the bloodstained hall. He thought of Branarius. Already these people, these *kings,* had acknowledged him leader in military matters. But—elsewhere? In their minds? Would these knees bend to him? Too, how long would he and Vidul be the military experts, with the knowledge of Nyor about to burst upon them all?

What was the best for Empire . . . for Branarius . . . for Aleysha . . . for himself?

There was no panacea. Something would have to be sacrificed. He realized that total rightness was not available to him, and so total happiness would not be. With a great silent sigh, he glanced about.

Imperial politics! Even the seating here was not haphazard. He had avoided the chair Saldon occupied to be away from Aleysha and so as not to seem to be presiding—and he had avoided the place at foot of table for the same reason; it faced her, and too the others might think he was attempting to call attention to himself . . . *Gods!* What involved thinking a man got into! What a pain was being civilized, and ruling! How miserable must be most of these crowned heads! That chair at table's foot—perhaps it was Lexton's place. But Lexton had done surprise on them all by bringing in Jheru and sitting at her side. Perhaps that place belonged to the new hero, Jallad. But Jallad was as near Aleysha as he could possibly get. Vidul? No, Vidul was a man apart already, and he was aware ot it.

We are both *men apart,* Valeron thought, scanning the table.

Across from Saldon, at Aleysha's right hand, sat Eshara. Beside her was Narran, with his fanatic's eyes and his twin-pointed beard and his silken robe of vermilion and gold-and-violet trim. Then there was Burgon of

Branarius, as uncomfortably out of place here as Jheru. Next him Vidul, somberly, studiedly black-clad amid the blaze of color and jewels of the others. On Vidul's right was Colonel Graylon of Maruthia, his eyes almost deifying the barbarian warlord across from him. The twelfth seat, at table's end—or alternate head?—had fallen to the great bulk of Narran's priest-aide, Abd ol-Haled, uncomfortable there until Valeron begun to ask his advice on matters of etiquette.

Politics, Valeron thought; subtle nuances were involved in everything, even positions at table. *Everyone,* he mused, *avoids the seat all feel to be presumptuous, and the new empress has not yet strength enough with her to award it.*

"Can you believe that once I was as muscular as you," Narran ol-Shalkh said. "Now my physicians mouth nonsense about my stomach crowding my heart or some such, and endangering my life! Beware, Valeron of Branarius! Beware the soft life, and love of food, and banquets such as this! You should do prayer that Branarius's mountains continue to provide you with enemies to keep you alert and fit!"

Valeron grinned, shaking his head. But behind that smile he frowned.

They had finished and were deep in their goblets of Nyor's most profitable export and a discussion of the day's events that carefully avoided mention of Jallad's weapon, when the empress stood.

She was beautiful. The necklace of the Seven Worlds gleamed and twinkled between her breasts, taut within the fitted bodice of her coronation gown. The seagreen mantle lay on her shoulders with her seafoam hair, and her waist was cinched by a wide gold belt with flashing jewels.

"I have had but little occasion to make speeches," the Empress Aleysha said, and she *was* empress now, and no longer Aleysha—or Leysha. "But . . . may I say that I am proud to be called empress by such monarchs as you. Jallad, Lexton, Valeron . . ." Her eyes moved down the table, while she called their names, one by one. "Vidul, Narran, Eshara . . . kings all, and what's more—fighters all. And the noble Burgon and Graylon: gentlemen of Branarius and Maruthia, I shall order medals struck for you, as Saviors of Empire. Our gathering is further ennobled by the presence of a son of Siense, Elder Saldon. Though she has been forced to leave us, I must make mention of our loyal Jheru, who guided my lord King Valeron hence to you all, and whose beauty again graces these halls."

Aleysha smiled, a brilliant burst of light, and nodded her head in a tiny, imperial bow. The Seven pearled pendant flashed on her bosom.

She is empress, Valeron thought, *every centimeter!*

"With such as yourselves guiding its worlds, Empire must rise to greater heights and achievements than ever before. King Jallad has told me of his Elders, trained Siensemen"—she bowed her head reverently with a glance at Saldon's dull robe—"searching endlessly for the old Knowledge, financed in their quest and their work by the royal treasury of Nyor. For which we must all be grateful," she added—and again that dark pall swirled about them.

They glanced, all of them, at the slim boy with his smooth chin and open face; the first Scientist in centuries.

"I warn you all," their youthful empress said, "that I shall call on you again and again for aid and advice. And let assurance by with you, too, that our Elders will visit your worlds in search of forgotten archives. Someday, and perhaps we ourselves shall see that day, we shall leave these chained worlds and go out among the stars to seek our cousins."

Saldon smiled. Across the table, Narran ol-Shalkh Premn IV frowned. Knowledge, misused knowledge of the Ancients, had angered the god Siense and had led to the Wrath, to destruction and the long slide into nighted barbarism and the long climb back. On Narran's hyperreligious world, Elders were priests only. Saldon was more, and Narran pretended not to see him.

Directly across from Shalkh, Jallad smiled. A rod of power . . . repaired airlock . . . the books and treatments and knowledge of illnesses and wounds . . . these were steps. Only steps, to be followed by more, lengthening into strides, forward . . .

There will be dissension, Valeron saw. *Aleysha's will be no easy path—and her husband's.*

They had been long at table; before anyone could give a toast to the empress, she called for entertainment, and abruptly the Warlord of Branarius excused himself. He was aware of their eyes, of *her* eyes, as he left the chamber.

He found her clear of tears, and said to her what had to be said, and she nodded, looking faint, biting her lips and keeping her eyes wide, and he returned to the hall of banqueting with the former Carmeian slavegirl.

The sweet-voiced singer ended her last note, and her fingers strummed a lingering chord. After a bow, she left them. Jallad rose, his handsome face flushed. He smiled that ingenuous boyish grin that had gained him so much.

"On behalf of Nyor, but most of all on behalf of myself, who have never seen so beautiful a woman on any world, I give you the long life and good health of the Empress of the Seven Worlds!"

The others joined in, rising and lifting their goblets as he did.

Aleysha turned to Jallad with a blinding smile, and bowed her head in pleasure. Studying her, Valeron saw her face darken with a worried little look of—what? Guilt? She bit her lip. She glanced at him and for a moment their eyes met at last; met and exchanged thoughts, and unspoken words, and meanings. He smiled, bowed his head as king to empress, and again he saw her sudden little frown.

"Aleysha, Empress of the Seven Worlds of Carmeis!" Eshara called, and again glittering cups swooped into the air and down to smiling lips.

Valeron's hand rose to rest lightly on Jheru's shoulder, gentle in its strength and yet over-strong in its attempt at gentleness. He leaned toward Jallad, lifting his cup to the King of Nyor.

"Good fortune, Jallad!" he said, and Jallad grinned and raised his own goblet in return salute.

Valeron's peripheral vision told him that Jheru was gazing only at her plate; beyond Jallad, Saldon's eyes narrowed while he searched his ruler's face. Valeron became aware that Eshara, neither ugly nor pretty but handsomely pathetic in her unwise mask of cosmetics, was addressing him.

"And what has the newest king to say to his peers?"

"And his followers," Lexton said.

"And his friends," Vidul added with a twisted grin, and instantly all eyes were on Valeron car Nadh, intent and waiting.

"Aye, my lord King Valeron," Aleysha said in a quiet, quiet voice. "We owe Empire—and our lives—to you, friend of my father."

She is giving me my opportunity, he thought. *Even with her uncertain new imperial "we" she is offering me my chance and right to say the words, to claim her and crown and throne, laying all at my door. A true woman, a true noble, a noble woman—a true empress. And—soft, by the gods, soft and pliant and over-yielding—it is in her delicate softness that she refuses to make a statement, cedes statement and her future to me! Darcus Cannu was right. She does need help, strength . . .*

He looked around on them, these twice-noble people who now called him peer. Consciousness was with him of their expectant looks, their wondering, their . . . apprehension? Valeron was aware that some of them, Lexton, and Eshara certainly—aye, and Vidul—realized the significance of this moment. Aleysha was passing to him the privilege of speaking, of claiming what her father's letter had offered.

What, he mused, *are you thinking, my lords and ladies, my peers? Follow a barbarian in combat, aye; follow him to victory as a natural combat leader. But . . . envision him in the palace? Darcus Cannu's words are with us all! Can vision be with you of what he crudely suggested: me abed with that petalsoft girl with the seafoaming tresses and the body that looks so breakable? Picture me, my lords and ladies, in those pale ultramarine robes?*

His former thought returned like an unforgettable curse: What was for the best of Empire, of Branarius, of Aleysha—of himself? And still the cure-all, the one decision that solved all, was not there.

Because he was a king, Valeron showed none of it.
He smiled.

"First I must say this: Elder Abd and I have insulted
the imperial table by remarking the sparsity of *salt*,
which I know is in short supply here. Along with the
Nyori wine, then, you shall soon pay good prices for a
valuable export from Branarius. Our mountains gleam
with white cliffs of salt, and no need will be with us to
mine for it for years. I am glad we have something to
offer in commerce." He laughed with them, and knew
all of them knew this was mere preface—though it was
good news, indeed.

"I fear that Branarius must continue to think of Siense as a god who withholds his graces; of the old
Knowledge as little more than unproven—and unprov-
able—legend. I fear that her ruler is a scarred warrior
with little knowledge of affairs other than war and tactics, and I thank the gods for the guidance of Elder
Saldon, without whom I could not be called king. And
I thank the gods too for Elder Abd here at my left, who
has guided me in the complicated table manners of the
capital."

He grinned and they smiled; Abd ol-Haled laughed,
jiggling from eyes to knees, and Lexton smilingly shook
his head while Jallad fidgeted and Valeron wondered:
*Still apprehensive, my lords and ladies? Still picturing
this edgeman's bulk and that wraith of an empress with
her slim hips? Still ready to follow me in war—unless it
be against Jallad!—but perhaps not now, in peace?*

*Oh what a Valeron would be on that great chair!
Have you thought of it, my noble fellow kings, my
peers? A strong hand on the rein of Empire again, a
young man, with the new understandings the Elders will
give us in the coming years? But do you laugh with me
because I have made a jest—that was no jest!—or from
unease because I speak truth and all know it? Wonder,
my lords and ladies. Wonder whether I make fun of myself . . . or of you!*

*For I, Valeron of the Barbarian World, am enjoying
myself!*

"Among you I am called 'king'. On my own world I

am called Warlord, a barbarous title for the leader of a barbarous people. To the brilliant Darcus Cannu—and perhaps a man can be too brilliant, too civilized?" He paused, letting them taste that like rust on their tongues, and then went on. "To the brilliant Darcus Cannu, I was 'my lord *Barbarian*.' I admit it. It is true. My world is a fierce one, with cliffs and mountains and deserts as fierce as its people, and I have perhaps little place in this .. civilized gathering. But—I invite and beg you to visit Branarius. I beg you not to leave Branarius in the past. I ask you to lend aid to Branarius, to send Elders to Branarius, as Jallad has promised ... for Branarius will have no ruler!"

Ah, now *they stare! Are those tears in your eyes, my fierce Burgon? Did you not know that if Lexton and I have my way you remain here, as Prefect of the Palatine Guard? Are your eyes perhaps a trifle too fixed, Your Eminence Aleysha?*

He held his pause again, relishing their looks, their shaking heads, the empress's confused—tortured?—expression.

She was Aleysha and now she is the Empress Aleysha, and between us now, he thought, *there is a yawning chasm; our eyes meet across a great distance, Empress, and now you've known the pleasant companionship of a civilized, noble, and doubtless brilliant boy your age. Can you see all that? Are you too much woman and not enough empress, Aleysha? Does she know her mind,* he wondered, and he answered himself: *Probably not.*

Then I must make it up for her.

"Branarius, I tell you, will have no ruler ... only poor Valeron the orphan, guided by Saldon. I return, my lords and ladies, to that barbarous world to build a capital city and a world fit to stand side by side with its fellow worlds. I take with me one ... *memento* ... of Carmeis."

He paused again, paused and grinned, barbarically delighted in the tense silence, deepened now by the new shock of his last words. *They have never seen,* he mused in pleasure, *a barbarous rock-cat of the mountains toy with his captive prey ...*

"The Sixth King has no queen to sit at his side, to

provide *legitimate* stout sons to hold Branarius and be future kings in council. When I leave here on the morrow, for you must do all this trying and sentencing and planning without me, my world needs me—I take my lady with me. I give you another toast, my lords and ladies . . . the Lady Jheru . . . *my* lady, Jehru."

Valeron listened to them, then, watched their wide-smiling faces, heard their overloud excited voices, as he stood with his big hands on the trembling warrior-woman with the delightfully round backside and great Branarian hips and swollen bosom and fierce temperament. He listened to them, avoiding Aleysha's eyes as she struggled within herself, then meeting them steadily, thinking with his barbarian's mind as he held his warrior-woman, his warrior's woman: *My dear friends! My noble peers! How relieved you all are!*

And they were.